MILLION DOLLAR DREAM

Giorgi had secretly adored Rafe all her life, but he was madly in love with — and destined to marry — her sister, Anna. But when Anna died, their fathers' dream to unite the two families and their wineries was thwarted . . . Will Giorgi marry Rafe, give up her city restaurant and return to the Australian Sunset company as his wife, knowing he doesn't love her? Or will she retain her independence, and deny any chance she may have had of happiness with him?

JO JAMES

MILLION DOLLAR DREAM

Complete and Unabridged

LINFORD
Leicester

First published in Great Britain in 2008

First Linford Edition
published 2008

British Library CIP Data

James, Jo
    Million dollar dream.—Large print ed.—
Linford romance library
1. Love stories
2. Large type books
I. Title
823.9′2 [F]

ISBN 978–1–84782–182–9

Published by
F. A. Thorpe (Publishing)
Anstey, Leicestershire

Set by Words & Graphics Ltd.
Anstey, Leicestershire
Printed and bound in Great Britain by
T. J. International Ltd., Padstow, Cornwall

Dedication

To my husband, Neil. His love and encouragement have enabled me to journey beyond the mountain.

Prologue

Full of enthusiasm and hope, youths Bruno Rintoli and Dominic Guardiani forsake their native land of Italy for Australia and plan their future. Their dream is to own vineyards, side by side, in the hot, Sunset Country of Victoria. And soon they taste success in the burgeoning Australian wine market. On the eve of Dom's marriage, they sit late into the evening at the old deal table in his home, drinking *vino* and dreaming another dream.

'We will have the *bambinos*. A son for you, a daughter for me,' Bruno says.

'Or a daughter for me and a son for you,' Dom adds with a gleam in his eye. 'And they will marry and have the *bambinos*, our grandchildren.'

1

Bruno holds his glass to Dom's. 'And then we will truly be one family.'

'Truly family,' they swear as one, their hearts full, their dream unquestioned.

1

Giorgi hated these winter late night returns from her restaurant. It was dark, cold and lonely as she hurried along the street to her house. The departing clatter of a tram at her back, her clicking heels reached into the silence.

Arriving at last at the terrace house, the sight of an unfamiliar off-road vehicle parked on the road sent her racing up the path to safety. The sensory light by the front door activated. Her breathing returned to normal. But, one foot on the verandah steps and she froze. Someone standing in the shadows watched her, his breath materializing into steam. Her heart slipped into overdrive.

'Who's there?' she demanded as a man emerged from the darkness.

He stood, framed in the evening

light, the collar of his coat turned up against the bleak Melbourne winter. Her heartbeat slowed. 'Rafe, you scared me. What on earth are you doing here?'

'Doesn't a guy who's traveled five hundred miles to see his best girl at least get a hug?'

Confused, uncertain, she brushed by him and unlocked the door. Lightening her tone, she said, 'Yes, if he's willing to wait until his best girl gets out of the cold.'

Inside, she waited for him to enter, using the few seconds to compose herself. 'I see you brought an overnight bag. You might have told me you were coming.'

'It's a spur of the moment visit. I can crash on the couch, if you've got one. Now about that hug.'

He reached out to her as she eased herself aside. 'First let me get my coat off, put a match to the fire,' she said. 'You *do* know it's the middle of the night?'

'Yep, so what? I'm here. Sorry, I can't

wait any longer. I've been planning this all the way down in the car.' His arms wrapped around her. She felt a slight prickling of a day's growth against her cheek, the strength of his body against her, its warmth. She tensed. Finally, he placed her at arm's length, his dark eyes seeking hers.

'It's so good to see you, little Giorgi. You look fantastic, even though you're a bit on the skinny side for a country girl. It's been too long since you've been home.'

Her heart in revolt, she lowered her eyes. 'I have my restaurant to run. I don't have the luxury of being able to get away whenever I feel like it.'

Which was only partly true. She'd needed to escape from the Sunset Country, and at great personal expense, had finally built a life for herself in bustling Melbourne. The thought of going home taunted her with memories; memories that flooded back the minute she'd seen Rafe on her verandah. Memories from which there was no escape while he lingered here.

'The fire,' she muttered. 'I should light it.'

'What's the matter, Giorgi? I thought you'd be pleased to see me. We were great mates back home, but now you're so . . . ,' he shrugged wide shoulders. 'You're kind of distant.'

She tried to laugh. 'Cut me some slack. I'm still getting over the surprise of seeing you.'

Conscious only of his footfalls behind her, she hurried into a small living room where a fire was laid in the grate. She placed a match to it, it crackled and spat briefly. When she turned back she dared a closer look at him. The unshaven, shadowed jaw and weariness around his eyes were obvious, but his dark beauty always had a strange effect on her. Even the room seemed to shrink in his presence.

'Sit down, Rafe,' she said, her tone almost a whisper. 'Take off your coat and sit down.'

He crossed to the fire and held his

hands toward the heat, rubbing them together. These were strong hands; hands which had once brushed away her tears. She lowered her glance to her own tightly clenched hands, trying to force herself to refocus on anything but him.

'Why would anyone want to live in a cold hole like Melbourne? You especially. At least at River Bend the days are sunny in winter.'

He sounded unnatural, harsh even, worried definitely. She couldn't see his face or his eyes, but she knew him so very well; his every movement, his every intonation. Not so long ago he had been engaged to her sister. Not so long ago their two families had dreamed of the day when Anna married Rafe; tall, lean, with a bounty of black hair and compelling dark-eyes which, when they softened, could melt the coldest heart.

But Anna was dead. The dream had turned to dust.

So why had he arrived so late and so unexpectedly on her doorstep when he knew his presence would only stir up the pain of the past?

She thought she knew the answer, but didn't risk pursuing it, unprepared yet to face the inevitability of it. Stay with the weather, it's safe, she told herself.

'At least Melbourne weather offers variety, Rafe. Those endless days of over one hundred degree heat aren't my idea of fun. Besides, my restaurant's starting to attract a regular clientele. It's exciting. You know there hasn't been anything for me in River Bend for a long time.'

He laughed mockingly. 'Giorgi, have your forgotten your heritage? Surely the future of our properties means something to you?'

She found it hard to talk about the vineyards where she'd been raised. She'd left six years ago to study business administration in Melbourne, and determined her future would be here. River Bend became the destination for holidays which she always cut short because in those days she'd felt like an outsider when around her sister and Rafe.

'I'm making coffee. Would you like a cup or would you prefer a drink?'

She started to leave for the kitchenette, expecting him to continue his lecture about her attitude to their birthplace, their adjoining properties, The Red Earth and Sunny Valley; expecting him to opt for a hot drink. She was wrong on both counts.

'There's something I want to ask you. Perhaps whiskey might be in order.'

She swung back, alarmed. 'Whiskey? It must be a very big ask.' She'd never known him to drink anything harder than wine and it confirmed what she dreaded. He was about to ask her the impossible.

'If you keep a bottle.' He dragged off his overcoat. She hurried across and took it from him.

His dark eyes were clouded, as if he couldn't see her, though he looked directly at her. 'Rafe, are you all right?'

'I'm tired.' He touched her arm, trying to smile. 'Do I get my drink?'

Her heart ached that she'd been so obvious in trying to avoid his hug — his touch — when throughout their childhood and growing up, they'd been as close as brother and sister; as dear and near to one another as two people could be.

He sank into the old sofa and stretched his legs, expelling a long, weary sigh.

'Why don't I make us a snack? Eggs? Toast?' Anything to quell her heartbeat; her suspicions as to why he'd come.

'I'll settle for the whiskey, thanks. Then, we should talk.'

Giorgi laid his coat across a chair, and with shaky hands, opened the sideboard, removing a bottle of brandy.

'Brandy's the best I can offer,' she said, pouring a small glass of the amber liquid. Perhaps she should have a drink herself? Goodness knows, she needed something to calm her. But as she reached for a second glass, she thought better of it. What she needed most was a clear head. She tilted her chin, determined not to let her over-zealous heart make decisions for her.

Handing him the drink, she sat down beside him, attempting to appear as natural as possible. For all of her 24 years, he'd appointed himself as her protector and confidante. He'd encouraged her with her career choices, persuading her reluctant father to allow her to move to the city for a tertiary education. Her peripheral vision told her he fiddled briefly with the brandy as if uncertain whether to drink it, before downing it in two gulps. She directed her gaze to the fire's flames, preparing herself. She'd been dreading this moment almost from the day they'd lost Anna. The knot in her stomach tightened. She took a long breath.

He reached across and took her hand. She lowered her eyes, afraid to meet his.

'Giorgi, will you marry me?' he

asked, his voice husky.

How could she marry him? Though she'd anticipated his proposal since his arrival, her heart leapt, her voice rising at the sound of the words. 'You don't know what you're asking.'

'Yes, Giorgi, I do. I want you to marry me.'

She didn't have the will or the courage to look into his eyes, or to say no and finish it there. She understood what it had cost him to ask, and why, indeed, he was prepared to pay that cost. Dragging her hand from his, she edged back in the sofa and found herself replying quietly, 'What hope would a loveless marriage have?'

He stood up, placing his glass on the mantle shelf over the fireplace as if buying time, before turning back to her. 'But you know I've always loved you, Giorgi.'

'And I've always loved you. But our kind of brother and sister love doesn't keep a marriage together. Be honest, Rafe. The love of your life was Anna and even if I took the chance, you'd forever be comparing me with her and what you've lost.'

Rafe stared down at her. How could he stain the memory she had of her sister by telling her the truth?

'I'm not asking you to replace Anna. I'm asking you to be my wife. My observations tell me that the key ingredients of a lasting marriage are love, loyalty and respect.' He dropped to his knees, taking both her hands in his. 'And we've always had those feelings for one another. Together we could make it work, sweet Giorgi. Come back to River Bend with me and be my wife.'

Troubled blue eyes stared back at him as she shrank back into the sofa. 'I can't,' she said, 'I can't. I just know it wouldn't work.'

He stood up, returning to the sofa and taking her hand. 'Of course it would. We'd make a great team. We have the power to reinvent the dream our fathers had to merge the two families and the wineries. Doesn't it excite you that you could make it happen? If your father were alive today, you know he'd give his blessing in a shot.' He tightened his fingers around her much smaller, softer hands, as if it might wring a yes from her.

'I can't go into a marriage when there isn't real love between us.'

'I'm not asking you to sleep with me, if that's what's worrying you.' He shrugged, 'Maybe later if . . . '

She wrested from his grip, surging to her feet. *That's not what's worrying me*, she almost shouted.

He stood, placing his hands around her waist, staring into misty blue eyes. 'Then what is it, little Giorgi?' he asked tenderly. 'Something's disturbing you. You don't normally cry for nothing.'

Quickly, her head fell. 'I'm not crying,' she protested.

'OK, I won't push it now, but sweetheart, I love you dearly, and I'm going to do everything within my power to persuade you to come back to the

Bend and be my wife. Please, promise you'll give my proposal serious thought?'

She nodded. He brushed aside a tendril of hair and folded her into his arms. 'Sweetheart, you're so cold. Let me build up the fire. I'll make you coffee.'

Gently he eased her back onto the sofa and turned to throw a few logs on the fire. 'You haven't got any muffins I suppose? We could toast them by the fire,' he said, trying to ease the tension.

He'd probably handled it insensitively, but he had so little experience to draw upon. His marriage to Anna had been preordained, written into the culture of their families. He'd never formally asked her to be his wife, though in bouts of impatience, of restless uncertainty, he had demanded a date from her.

'I don't know what's in the fridge. I'll have a look,' she said, rising.

'Stay there. Let me do it.'

'I need to be busy.' She brushed by him.

She was right, of course. She nearly always was. He'd ambushed her with his proposal, and thinking and doing other things might help her cope with the shock.

'I'll never understand how you can live in this little place when you come from God's own country. There's hardly room to open even a tacky little tabloid, and how you can breathe out there in the streets . . . '

He'd succeeded in reviving her spirits.

'My money's in the restaurant. This little terrace isn't flash, but it's comfortable and affordable,' she said with force. 'Besides . . . '

Giorgi was about to lie and say she preferred inner-city living to the vast, vivid reds and blues of the River Bend landscape, the ancient river gums of her home, when he interrupted.

'Nonsense.' His mood changed as if at the switch of a lever. 'You were your father's only heir. You haven't forgotten that you own the Red Earth, have you,

16

Giorgi? You could walk out of this forgettable little apology for home tomorrow.' He railed as he followed her into the kitchen.

In a sense, she welcomed his flare-up — for it sparked the feeling of frustration which lingered beneath her battle to stay cool.

'Do you mind? This is my home, and if you don't like it you're free to leave any time. Agreed, it isn't poshville, and it doesn't match the palace you've built at River Bend, but it suits me just fine.'

She'd always loved his eyes. Sometimes they held gentle warmth; sometimes the fire of passion when he spoke of his love of The Bend. Now as they looked down at her, she saw only loneliness, a heart-rending emptiness in their depths. And it confirmed again, as if it needed confirmation, how much losing Anna had affected him.

'You know I built that house for your sister. Anna wanted it, not me. She designed it. She furnished it.' He flourished his hands. 'And now, I can't . . . I can't go anywhere near it without getting screwed up inside.' His voice rose as he ran both hands through his thick, bible-black hair, dislodging it to fall with abandon across his forehead.

In films, she'd watched women run their fingers through their lovers' dark, lustrous hair with a tug of envy. A sudden wild urge to go to Rafe, to comfort him, welled inside her. But she gripped the edge of the door, her knuckles white with determination, and murmured, 'I shouldn't have mentioned it. It was thoughtless. What do you plan to do with the place?'

'I've got too much else on my mind for now. It will go on the market when I get around to it.'

'You're not living there, Rafe?'

'I'm back at Sunny Valley. Only it isn't sunny any more.' He gave a hollow laugh. 'Pa's still pretty shell-shocked. He needs me around. Besides, it's easier to manage the property while I'm living there.'

'Pa Dom isn't any better? I thought with time . . . '

'Time? It's a cliché', Giorgi. The healing is not happening at the Valley. He's a broken old man. He's lost his lifelong friend, and Anna. I don't have to remind you your father and he were closer than brothers, and Anna was as dear to him as the daughter he never had.'

No, she didn't need any reminding. *Anna meant everything to everyone. Sometimes it felt as if I wasn't there.* But all she said quietly was, 'I know.'

'You, too,' he added as if realizing his mistake of omission and adding the afterthought.

'Whatever.' She pushed into the kitchen, weary of the memories.

But Rafe went on. 'Whatever?' he demanded. 'Pa and Bruno's dream of bringing their families and their two vineyards under the one title is in tatters. Sometimes I wonder if you quite understand what we've all lost.'

Giorgi stared at him, her eyes

threatening to mist up. 'Bruno was my father, and Anna my sister, and you don't think I care that they're dead? How could you be so insensitive? I lost the only two people in my family in . . . in one . . . ' She closed her eyes, forcing back tears. 'In one tragic night, and you accuse me of not understanding.'

Determined against tears, she paused, dragging out the words, 'Excuse me, I'm going to make a sandwich. I'm hungry.'

He followed her across to the sink. 'Sorry, I've been a thoughtless wretch.'

She heard the useless apology above thumping down the toaster on the sink, stabbing the plug into the socket, clattering in the cupboard for plates and mugs, filling the kettle. Her thoughts ran rampant.

All her life everyone assumed she had a mental toughness which enabled her to glide over the rough bumps in life; a willful streak that made her put her own needs before everyone else's. But they were wrong. After Anna and her father died in the motor accident, her vulnerability often surfaced. Only she knew of the sadness, of the desolation, like the deep, resonant notes of a cello, which plucked at her heart. Losing them had also compelled her to question her friendship with Rafe. She had decided it would be folly to allow it to continue.

The soft pads of her fingers burned as she rescued a forgotten slice of blackened bread from the toaster.

'You need a man around the house.' He stood by the pantry, a hint of a smile on his lips. 'You're such an impractical, stubborn little . . . '

She broke in. 'Don't you dare call me a stubborn little dude. That nickname is well beyond its used-by-date. And what I need more than a man right now is an automatic toaster.' Forcing a laugh, she seized a knife and began scraping the burnt toast into the sink, aware from the tone of his voice that his mood had lightened. Hopefully the brandy had started to unwind the coil of anger within him.

'But it described you so well — game, affectionate, generous. And you always laughed when I called you that. Come on, you loved it.'

She pointed to her face, controlling an untimely urge to go soft at the memories he'd evoked. 'Do you see me laughing now that I'm a successful business woman?'

Two steps in the tiny cooking area and he stood beside her, reaching out to her. 'Giorgi, about losing Anna and Bruno, I didn't mean to imply . . . '

She felt his hands on her shoulders but steeled herself to continue scraping away at the toast. 'What? That I've got a cold heart?'

'Will you stop that damned scratching? I'm trying to apologize.'

She dropped the charred bread into the sink as she faced him with defiant 'see if I care' eyes. 'Apology accepted.'

'You could have fooled me.' In the

small area his voice rang with exaspera-
tion. 'Of course you felt the loss of your
pa and sister, but you're strong,
resilient, young — and you've got your
life going in the right direction. My old
man's devastated. Everything up there
reminds us of what might have been, of
what we've lost.' His voice slowed.
'Down here you're away from all the
memories.'

'I can't follow your reasoning. Not
five minutes ago, you told me I should
come back to River Bend. You're not
making any sense.' He was, of course.
She understood his meaning very well,
but to acknowledge it, to surrender to
her feelings would bring on a rush of
tears again.

'You know I was making the point
that this dark, dingy little place with a
kitchen no bigger than a closet, can't
compare with the space and light of
home. Up there you'd have a toaster
which automatically toasted ten slices if
that's what you wanted. Next time I
visit I'll bring you one.'

'In the middle of the night? Sometime? Never?' she scoffed, waving the knife in one hand. 'Don't bother, I'll get one tomorrow.'

Smiling, he dodged to her side, his arms and fists poised in a boxing gesture.

She laughed.

'What a good idea. Tomorrow, little dude, we'll go shopping. And, for pity's sake put down that knife. You look so dangerous.'

He unwound her fingers from the handle of the knife. His breath whispered across her cheek, the warmth of his touch filling her with desire. If she reached up, her lips could find his.

Dear heaven, what was she thinking? He was her friend, her sister's lover. The knife, as it fell into the dish drainer, clattered in tune with her heart.

'You amaze me. You run a restaurant, yet you can't even make a decent piece of toast. I pity your poor customers. Stand aside. Let me show you how it's done.'

She took a long breath. Apparently he could no longer read her thoughts. As she stepped aside and watched his every movement with a rebellious heart, he took two slices from the bread packet and shoved them under the stove griller.

'Clever you,' she mocked. 'By the way, I own and run the restaurant. I greet the clients, take the bookings, order the food, balance the books — I'm the business manager. I don't work in the kitchen. I employ a chef to handle that.'

'And does the business manager have anything as practical as a box of matches to light the gas?' His eyes ranged around the area of the stove.

It brought a smile to her lips. 'You don't need matches. The stove has automatic ignition. See,' she added, tilting one brow. 'I do have some mod cons.'

'But do they work?' He found the button, pressing it a couple of times without response.

She laughed, grateful for the moment of levity. 'I suggest you need more training with mod cons. First, you have to turn on the gas.'

He returned his attention to the stove, and soon a tiny explosive sound told her the griller was alight. A grin eased the contours of his face as he glanced across at her. For the first time since he'd arrived on her doorstep he looked relaxed. The Rafe of her growing-up days. Halcyon days.

A few years younger than her sister, she'd been born a girl, instead of the boy her father longed for. And, unlike her sister, was solid, sturdy with hair that refused to curl, and according to her Momma, blue eyes which glinted with defiance.

She'd longed to be loved and petted and fussed over as Anna was. She'd sought to say and do things to please her family, but try as she may, she couldn't grasp exactly what they expected of her.

Only Rafe accepted her free spirit.

She was around eight when he'd found her down by the river, crying. It hadn't taken much coaxing for her to blurt out, 'It isn't fair. I wish I were a boy like Papa wanted. My family hates me.'

Rafe had hugged her, called her a great little dude and said if she wasn't around, all their lives would be awfully dull. He'd lifted a tear from her face with his index finger, tapped her across her nose and grinned. 'You've sure got a pert little nose, Giorgi.'

She'd smiled through her tears, raced home to look up 'pert' in the dictionary, and discovered it wasn't the compliment she'd hoped for, such as pretty or lovely. But because he'd said it, she consoled herself with the thought that 'pert' was something special, and who'd want to be pretty when you were special?

From that day, he'd looked out for her, a sorcerer, sensing when she needed reassurance and support, a peacemaker, urging Anna to let her join in their activities.

'Giorgi,' she heard him say quietly through a mist of thoughts, 'when will you have an answer for me? I said I wouldn't push you, but we're wasting time here and the suspense is killing me. I want to get back to Pa and tell him . . .'

He stood beside her, so close a prickly heat stung her body. The temptation to say yes and be damned to the consequences, trembled with uncertainty on her lips. It could work — her heart had begun to have its way — until the words, *You don't have to sleep with me*, flashed in her mind like a bold, warning headline. And she knew with an innate assurance it wouldn't work.

'The toast is burning,' she said, thankful for the interruption, as she reached for the toaster tray. The sound of water gushing into the sink partly filled the awkward silence between them. She used her fingers to swish the burnt fragments from the toast down the outlet. What would she say? How would she cushion her reply?

'Our whole future is at stake here and you're bothered about a bit of burnt toast?' His voice rose with impatience.

'And you're crowding me when you promised you'd give me time.'

'You've had at least half an hour. A man likes to get things done. What's the point in waiting?' he demanded.

Rafe watched her dry her fingers on a towel, twist them into a tight knot and settle them in front of her flat stomach. He saw the anguish in blue eyes that always mirrored her moods. Over the years, he'd read those eyes better than anyone.

Sometimes I'm scared to look at you, she once told him. You tap into my feelings. I can't have you knowing my innermost secrets.

He thought he understood her hesitation. He should have laid the groundwork, been more patient. But no — he'd blurted out the proposal; blurted out his insistence on an answer when he'd promised her time. It was the Guardiani hot-headedness at its best.

29

Problem was he'd almost lost his nerve when he saw her in the half-light; her short, dark hair clipped behind one ear, a sheen on one high cheek bone, and eyes wide with surprise. She'd looked so fragile, yet so controlled.

She'd begun to have that strange, ambivalent affect on him after she reached her teens, when her once plump, cuddly little body, gave way to slim, shapely curves. When her mischievous blue eyes were no longer a cause for ribbing, but a light source of her moods. The tough little dude was growing into an attractive woman of independence and purpose.

'A woman likes to plan things, do them properly.' Her voice, little more than a whisper, pulled him back to the moment.

'What's not proper about us getting married?'

'I didn't say it was improper, but I don't get asked to be someone's wife every day.'

He placed his hands on her shoulders, grasping her firmly. He felt a tremor ripple through her at his touch.

'I've caught you by surprise, but you've had half an hour to consider it. Will you marry me?' he asked, trying to calm the devil of impatience within.

She looked up at him, her blue eyes clearer and he thought, as a knot settled in his gut, she'd decided. Anxious fingers bit into her soft flesh, but when she lowered her gaze, the knot in his stomach tightened.

He had lost, wasted his time coming here. She was about to turn him down.

'I need time to process all this. Ask me again in twelve months.' She sounded calm enough, but he could feel the tension in her shoulders.

And he could hear the derision in his laughter, the despair in his own voice. 'Twelve months? You've got to be joking. It'll be too late. We'll have lost everything by then.' She flinched, trying to shrug off his grip, but he held her still.

'You're letting your emotions run away with you, Rafe.' With an effective twist she freed her body from his hold.

'You're right. I'm emotional and don't expect an apology for it. You've lived all your life with our fathers' dream to unite the Red Earth and Sunny Valley under one ownership. Are you going to spit on the opportunity you've been given to reinvent that dream when all it requires is for you to marry me? Am I such a turn off to you?' He reached across to her with his eyes. 'Is that really how little you care?'

Her eyes filled with tears. He saw his advantage and moved quickly, tilting her chin, compelling her to look directly into his eyes. 'Little Giorgi, can you deny two old men their lifetime wish? Please, make their dream live again in my father's heart. Think of it, you and me, we can defy fate and make it happen. You and me together.'

2

Giorgi stared up at him. 'You can't play God, Rafe. Has it never occurred to you that perhaps the dream wasn't meant to be?'

Anger ate away at what little control he still had, pushing him on, though he knew his approach was wrong; he knew he was being unfair to her. 'I'm not trying to play God. I'm trying to be practical. I don't think you have any idea of what's happening up there. We could lose everything if we don't merge the two properties.'

'I don't follow,' she said quietly, easing his finger from her chin, dashing her hand across her eyes.

'The wine industry has become huge in Australia, a major export business. I'm not telling you anything you don't know. What you probably haven't realized is that our two small enterprises are being eyed-off by bigger players. With the mortgages on our properties, we're sitting ducks for a takeover.'

He flourished his hands. 'It's up to you, Giorgi. If you marry me, we could combine our holdings into a fine showpiece as our fathers planned, one the millionaires can't touch. Doesn't that excite you?'

'Please,' Giorgi said, with a strength and irrelevance which further inflamed his anger, 'this is too small a room for you to be shouting.'

'Every poky room in this apology for a house is too small for shouting, but I have to shout to make you understand how vital this is.'

'And you've chosen to make me see things your way by shouting at me? Impressive,' she snapped.

Hell, how could I be so gross? He strode towards the door, knowing he had to get out of the room before he did more damage to his case.

'It's hellishly cold in here. I'm going back to the fire. Coming?' he muttered at the entrance.

'Only if you tone down. Next thing we know the police will be knocking on the door charging us with disturbing the peace.'

He couldn't see her eyes, but her voice suggested she was trying to ease the tension.

What a cool, independent lady she'd become. She no longer needed his reassurance, or came to him for advice. She'd effectively locked him out of her life — and, God help him — he didn't like it. But what really upset him was he didn't understand why.

Anna had been so different. She leaned on him, needed him for his stability, the security he offered, his strength to rescue her from the scrapes she so often got into. For a girl from River Bend, she'd learned very fast how to use credit cards, how to get on to the mailing lists of overseas high-fashion catalogues, where to find the expensive boutiques in Melbourne, and how attractive she was to other men.

He'd always suspected she didn't love

him deeply, but she'd never objected to the marriage plan. And he loved her for putting the family first. Until that last night.

He hit his head with the palm of his hand. Why on earth was he thinking about that now? Anna was dead. His only goal, his only reason for getting up every morning, was to keep the properties viable and in the Guardiani and Rintoli names.

If he didn't succeed . . . Though he felt cold, beads of sweat broke out on his forehead. Hastily, he mopped them up with a handkerchief. Two people could play at being cool, he assured himself.

He heard the door to the kitchen close as he slumped onto the sofa.

When she came in, he'd better have something calm and positive to say, or she might turf him out; and his impulsive five hundred plus miles journey would have been a waste of time.

'It's safe to come in,' he said when he

noticed her, hesitant, at the door. 'The savage beast's breast has calmed.'

'How generous of you . . . ,' a smile lingered on her lips, ' . . . to invite me into my own sitting room.'

She'd always had a way of saying things, a knack he supposed, of relieving the tension. And there'd been plenty of it over the years at their two properties.

'You haven't lost your touch,' he said, returning her smile. 'I wonder how many squabbles you managed to avoid between Pa and Bruno with your stringent little asides?'

'Nobody could take their heated words seriously. They were joined at the hip, those two.' She made her way to the fire, taking a couple of logs from the basket and tossing them into the flames.

As she bent over, he thought, *trim hips, nice little butt*. How could he not notice? He was a man.

She turned back to him. 'You've inherited your quick temper from your dad. You get steamed up easily and cool down just as quickly. A bit of ranting and raving can be positively affirming I always think.'

He laughed. 'The old Italian hot blood coming out, eh?'

Smiling, she sat on a chair close to the fire, linked her fingers and held his gaze with slightly narrowed eyes. He guessed she was about to say something important.

'Perhaps that's as good a reason as any for me to refuse your proposal of marriage? Think of the verbals we could get into.'

'You're not hot blooded. With your sea blue eyes and cool manner, I sometimes wonder if you have any Italian blood in you.'

'Have you forgotten I had an Australian momma? I take after her.'

'Valda? You're not in the least like her. She had a breezy, carefree attitude to life. Anna took after her. You . . . '

Giorgi's eyes shadowed.

He'd been clumsy with his remarks.

If only he could take them back. He hadn't meant to compare her with Anna, yet he felt vaguely pleased at her reaction. Seldom did her strength desert her, but suddenly she'd become the uncertain child in need of him, and the alchemy of his reassurance.

He gave her what he thought she needed. 'You, Giorgi, are like yourself, an individual, one of-a-kind, very special.'

'Are you trying to sweet talk me into something, Mr Guardiani?' Her eyes glinted. 'For example, becoming Mrs Guardiani,' she added with a curve of her lips.

'I mean it. I've always regarded you as special, different. Our friendship is special. I have the greatest respect for you. I enjoy being with you. That's why this marriage could work. Is it so hard to say yes, Giorgi? We can make it. I know we can.' Rafe edged forward on the sofa, an eagerness in his heart, his feet firm on the worn carpet. Should he reach for her hands, make some physical gesture towards her?

Giorgi felt a stab of pain where her heart beat. Who wanted a proposal high on principals and compromise and low on love and romance? Did he think she was a robot to whom he could say patronizing words such as 'you did it for the family,' and 'thank you. I couldn't run the place without you,' at the end of each day. And then disappear into his bedroom, telling her he'd see her in the morning?

With a rush of certainty she knew his terms would never work for her. They'd be living a lie. And yet, there was the matter of the merger of the two vineyards. Could she blindly ignore the fact that the wineries could be taken over by big time players whose only love for the business was the profit it brought them? That they would thumb their nose at the idealistic dream of two honest, hard-working migrants who had loved and embraced Australia?

The compelling thought had her appealing to Rafe, 'Please try to understand. This is about as hard as it gets for me, but to marry you would be wrong for both of us. There has to be another way. I could sign over my rights to the Red Earth so that you own both properties.'

He slumped back into the sofa, laughing mockingly. 'That wouldn't solve anything. You think I'd let you give away your father's years of sweat and toil as if they were some prize in a magazine competition?'

'But it would stay in the family — you've always been family — and solve the takeover problem.'

'Giorgi, surely you're not serious.' His voice rose. 'You know as well as I do that part of the dream was for the two families to merge as well. That was implicit in their plan, so you can forget any thought of handing the place over to me.'

'You're getting excited again.'

His hands shot up, his palms facing her, as if to ward off the words. 'I'll get emotional if I want to. And for someone with a business degree, you're being impractical. I will not let you give away your birthright. Got it?'

'You could pay it off in manageable installments. If it helps you feel any better, make a down payment now, and buy me out in your own time. I'm not in any hurry for the money. My restaurant is starting to do well.'

Again he laughed, even more harshly. 'Buying Bruno's place on hire purchase? Not likely. Your pa worked his guts out to build up his vineyard for his kids. He'd turn in his grave if he heard what you're proposing. And Dom would agree with me. More than anything they wanted us to be a real family.'

'I think you're wrong. His first priority would be to keep the properties together, no matter what it took.' She argued convincingly, but knew in her heart Rafe was right. Her father wouldn't want his beloved Red Earth given up so easily. The plan had always been for both families to become one, to share the fruits of the old men's labors.

'There's only one sensible solution to the problem, and that's for us to get married. It's the bottom line.'

As she looked into dark, hopeful eyes, watching him brush his hair back from his forehead with strong hands, her heart yearned to say yes. Quickly, she turned away, fearful of the temptation, the stirring in her body. Escape was all she could think about; escape from the pressure of his presence; escape to where her thoughts could run free.

She manufactured a yawn. 'I'm tired, you're tired. The morning light will soon be here. Why don't we sleep on it?'

A sinking feeling developed in her stomach as the word 'sleep' echoed teasingly through her head. *You don't have to sleep with me*, he'd said.

A marriage to Rafe hadn't a hope in hell.

To her relief he seemed content with her suggestion. 'Where do I crash?'

She shrugged, indicating the sofa with a wave of her hand. 'All I can offer is this and some warm blankets.'

'I take it you have no spare rooms in your trendy little city house?'

She ignored his taunt. 'I'll bring you some pillows and blankets.'

'Thanks,' he muttered, shrugging broad shoulders, displaying hands that forcefully suggested he felt only frustration and weariness.

As she went out to the linen press, a smile touched her lips. She had a sudden image of his long legs hanging over the edge of the sofa. He was in for a very uncomfortable night. Her thoughts ran on. Often she'd fallen asleep on the sofa, exhausted after a long night at her restaurant, and found it quite comfortable. Should she offer him the bed? *Don't be a softie. You've been at work all night, besides, it's his own fault for arriving so late. He should have told you he was coming.*

As she searched through the cupboard for bedding, in the background she heard him moving about the house, but when she returned, clutching sheets and blankets, she found the sitting room empty. He was probably in the kitchen or bathroom.

She stoked the fire, placed the guard around it, made up the bed on the sofa, and yawning, went looking for him. He wasn't in the kitchen. She called his name, but received no answer. Perhaps he'd gone out to his vehicle to collect something. Yawning almost incessantly, she decided she couldn't wait any longer to get to sleep. Entering her bedroom, she closed the door on a huge sigh, and switched on the light.

When she saw him slumped on top of the big bed, still wearing his heavy, roll-necked pullover and elastic-sided boots, she opened her mouth to demand, 'What on earth do you think you're ... ' But his peaceful, steady breathing silenced the words in her throat. Her heart softened. He must have been out before his head touched the pillow. Tip-toeing to his side, she gently eased off his boots and covered him with the duvet.

Normally, she'd have metaphorically thrown out anyone who so loftily took over her bed — not that it had ever happened, she reminded herself, briefly amused — but it was easy to make excuses for him. He'd probably done a day's work before he'd left River Bend for the long drive. Besides, she reasoned, after a good night's rest, he'd understand he was asking too much of her and return home without much fuss.

She gazed down at his sleeping figure, touched by tenderness, a desire to place her lips to his eyes, to his cheek, and knew with an unquestioning certainty what a travesty any marriage to him would be.

She loved him too deeply — had loved his gentleness, his thoughtfulness, his honesty, his dark beauty for a lifetime. Hopelessly. And now fate offered her a chance to be his wife.

She shivered. Of course he would

never truly be hers as he had been Anna's. At night she'd go to a cold, empty bed and lay there wondering where he was, who he was with. She'd wrestle with a longing to be with him, and betray her love by sometimes succumbing to his love-making for the physical high he sought.

As she turned away — bone weary, desolate — the bed, which took up most of the small room, ambushed her attention. How warm and tempting it looked. In a fog of fatigue, crazy thoughts filtered through her head. Rafe was deep in sleep. Why not crawl in and curl into a tight ball on one side? He wouldn't even stir.

And come the morning? She'd set her wrist alarm to ensure she woke before him. She stopped thinking, turned out the light, dropped her clothes to the floor, and slowly raised the spare pillow. Stilling nervous fingers, she slid a brushed cotton shirt from under it, and slipped it over her head. Shivering now, she slowly lifted the edge of the duvet.

Her fingers stalled, she froze when he stirred. 'Why, Anna, why?' he murmured. Her breath caught in her throat, her body tensed but she dare not move. His breathing settled back into a steady pattern.

Her exhaustion fell away as would a heavy cloak from slumped shoulders. She made it back to the sitting room in Olympian time, his anguished question tearing at her heart. Anna would always be there between them. Always had been.

She built up the fire, her hands icy, and stood toasting her body, unable to stop shivering, unable to motivate herself. Finally, she crawled under the blankets on the sofa. If she hadn't been so brain-dead weary she would never have had the wild idea to get into the same bed as a man who didn't love her. It was her last thought before she slept.

★ ★ ★

A ray of light filtered through the lace curtain over the small side window. Enough to wake Giorgi. She stretched her arms above her head, gingerly moving her feet to the floor and shivering. 'Bother,' she muttered, glancing at her watch. It was already after eight. She must have slept through the alarm.

Springing to her feet she remembered Rafe had commandeered her bed. Should she give him a hard time over it and send him back to the Bend with a decisive, non-negotiable 'No' ringing in his ears? What choice did she have?

Her university friends, in whom she'd confided her love for Rafe, would look incredulous if she told them she'd refused his proposal because he didn't love her. They'd probably suggest she see a therapist. They'd certainly say, 'It's not too late to entice him into bed. Get him alone, soften him up with a few drinks, wear sexy underwear, put on some mood music and try a little candlelight. He's always been half in love with you by the sound of it, so if you really want him, fight for him. Make it happen.'

Dare she risk it? For goodness sake stop prevaricating. He'd made it very clear it would be a marriage of convenience. Sure, there would be moments of physical weakness when he'd want her. But she'd always know afterwards that all he'd given her was his heated body.

His heart, his soul belonged to Anna.

And what if he guessed after sleeping with her that she loved him? He'd feel compassion, sympathy for her. Dear heaven, she thought, as a shudder scudded through her, she'd rather have his scorn, his coldness, than his pity.

Draping a blanket around her shoulders, she crossed to the fireplace and raked over the ashes with the poker. Not a single ember; not a glimmer of hope. Shaking, she wrapped the blanket more firmly about her and went in search of newspaper and kindling to restart the fire. As she crept down the narrow passage on icy feet, her thoughts returned to the big bed, to being curled up bedside him, warmed by his body and her pulsing heart. But determination carried her beyond the open bedroom door without a sideways glance.

At the back entrance, she had a shaky hand on the knob when she heard someone moving around outside. Silently, she edged open the door. A mist hung over the entrance, but there was no mistaking his silhouette by the old garden shed. In haste, clutching the blanket to her, she retraced her footsteps, but when she heard the backdoor open, she paused, one foot suspended, hardly daring to breathe.

'Going somewhere?'

Though she half-expected it, his voice seemed to boom through the empty passage. 'I hope you slept well, Giorgi.'

She swung to face him, steadying herself against the wall, ready to pay out on him for taking over her bed; for stuffing up her plans for the future. But when she saw him, a moment of breathlessness overwhelmed her. His shirt sleeves rolled to his elbows, sweat on his brow, his hair flaunted across his forehead, he carried an armful of wood.

'You were sleeping so soundly I decided not to disturb you. I wanted to surprise you with a warm fire. As I expected, no wood. So I've chopped enough for a few days.'

She clipped hair behind one ear. She probably looked a sight. 'You saw me? You came into the sitting room and saw me asleep?'

'You sleep with your mouth open.' He grinned, pushing by her.

He smelled sweaty, male. 'Do not.' She dragged the blanket around her, trailing him back to the sitting room.

'You haven't seen yourself asleep, little dude, so let's not argue about it.'

'I asked you before not to call me that. Pa hated that name. He called it too American.'

'The Americans coined it, but everybody used it, just like everybody wears baseball caps today. Anyway you liked it at the time. That's what matters to me.'

She stood in the doorway of the lounge, her cold fingers aching from clutching the blanket.

'Dude is so out these days.'

He laughed. 'And you're so busy being a today's woman?'

Once being his little dude had meant everything to her. Even now she admitted a responsive stirring in her heart when he said it, a flash of happy memories, an almost wistful longing to go back and live the time again. She tossed her hair back from her cheek, trying to concentrate on watching him set the fire.

'Yes, if owning and running a restaurant equates to being a today's woman.' As she said it she couldn't escape the thought that her personal life would never earn her a tick of approval from him. His presence, his practical skills, only emphasized her lack of a social life; her shortcomings as an Italian homemaker. The woman who married Rafe would run the household — no career, no discussion, no arguments. It was the Italian way and it had driven her mother away from River Bend and its tight-knit traditions.

Giorgi had once asked Anna what she planned to do after her marriage. Her sister had shrugged and laughed mockingly. 'They call it household duties, and delivering *bambinos*. I call it Dullsville.'

'But you organize excellent parties and things, and to have Rafe's child . . . ' Giorgi had protested.

'He's not god, Giorgi. He's only a man.' Anna had tossed it off with a smile on her lips.

The heat had flushed across Giorgi's cheeks. She'd turned away, biting on her lip.

'Matches, or does your grate have electronic ignition, too?' His jibe lanced into her thoughts.

'On the mantel shelf.' About to

indicate with one arm when the blanket started falling away from her shoulder, she hastily changed her mind, dragging the cover back into place.

He stood up, reached for the match box and began whistling a lively tune — 'I've Been Everywhere, Man'. For some reason the words translated in her mind to, 'I'm Not Going there, Man'. She was being negative. She forced a wide smile, determined on livening up. 'You must have had a good night's rest. You sound happy.'

'And positive.'

Have I missed something here? she needed to ask, needed to know. But she shrugged off the question, telling herself not to get too eager. She'd find out soon enough.

As he crouched beside the fire, his broad shoulders hid the grate completely, but she soon heard the light wood spark and spit as the dancing flames illuminated part of the room. She hurried across to warm herself.

'There's something comforting about

a fire,' she murmured. He moved aside on his haunches to make room for her.

'Remember the big logs on the fires at home, the kettle boiling on the hearth . . . ? Wonderful. Doesn't it make you long to be back at the Bend?' He rose, appraising her.

There was something sensual about the dark, unshaven jaw; the muscled forearms; the disheveled hair and crumpled clothes. Giorgi's heart took a leap into the unknown and came back with a swift jerk, pounding wildly. Instinctively she thought escape, but where to? There was no escape from Rafe. He would always be there — part of her.

'It sounds lovely.' She sat on the edge of a chair by the grate, leaning towards the fire. A shiver ran through her body.

'You're frozen.' He gazed down at her, the look in his eyes soft and gentle, the old caring Rafe. 'Stay here, Giorgi, and get warm. I'll make breakfast.'

'I'd best get dressed first,' she muttered.

'I noticed your clothes littered around the bedroom. Got undressed in a hurry?'

She stood up. 'I wasn't expecting to find you in my bed.'

'I don't think I apologized for that? As I remember it, I was on my way back from the bathroom, glanced into the bedroom. I swear to you, that bed fairly beckoned to me. I can't remember anything else after that.'

'You sleep with your mouth open, too.' She smiled. *Payback time*.

'We make a good couple don't we?' He placed his hands on her shoulders. The blanket shifted alarmingly. She pulled away, running her tongue over dry lips. 'I know what you're trying to do. And it won't work.'

'So how *can* I get the green light? Tell me, sweetheart.'

She dragged the blanket closer to her. 'You're wasting your time, losing my trust. I'm looking for a hidden agenda in everything you do and say.'

'I want you to marry me. What's

hidden about that? You shy away from me whenever I get close. If that's what's worrying you, you have my word. I won't make any physical demands on you. Later, once the merger's legally tied up, if things aren't working out for us, I'll give you your freedom. It need take only as long as that. Six months, a year at most.'

It sounded colder than her bare feet. She shuddered. 'You'd put our marriage vows aside that easily?'

'I wasn't thinking of a church wedding. I had in mind something down here, a quiet service with a celebrant. The more I think about it, the more it makes sense to go home as man and wife. That way we avoid all the trappings of an Italian extravaganza with the six-tiered cake and full orchestra. Don't you agree?'

She turned away, angry. 'It's not how I'd want to get married. I'd better get some clothes on before I freeze to death.'

As she hurried to the bedroom, he

called, 'Put on some warm gear. We're going shopping after breakfast. As well as the pop-up toaster, we're buying a couple of decent electric heaters, and a few other things. They'll be handy for the new tenants of this place when we go home to the Bend.'

He'd taken over her life, made all the plans, sounded so sure of himself. She began to wonder if he hadn't arrived last night, expecting her to fall into his arms and agree to marry him without so much as a murmur.

He'd intimated his trip was spur-of-the-moment, but it had all the hallmarks of a well-planned assault, including the fact that he'd brought an overnight bag, ready to stay on and assist her to vacate her house. He'd always been open — another one of the traits she'd admired in him — but he *had* timed his arrival to perfection. Could he have known she closed her restaurant at eleven on Sunday evenings, and didn't reopen to clients until Friday for lunch? That she had several free days ahead of her?

Time for him to persuade her?

Alas, she thought with a swell of sadness, given all the time in the world she mustn't allow herself to fall under his spell and agree to the marriage.

3

Rafe moved the sofa back from the fire, placed the sheepskin rug in front of it, and brought the coffee table closer. In the kitchen, he turned on the percolator, found a packet of muffins in the refrigerator, and set up a tray with butter, honey, mugs, plates and knives.

He'd expected some resistance from Giorgi. She was her own woman; had to be convinced about the rights and wrongs before she made weighty decisions. But in the past she'd listened to his advice and generally accepted it. Surely she could see the benefits that their marriage would bring.

The two families had lived with the phrase, 'the million-dollar merger', ringing in their ears for what seemed an eternity. As they grew older the children jokingly changed it to 'the million dollar dream', and teased their fathers. Dom and Bruno, who had migrated to Australia as youths, and struggled to build the two estates from the dry, red earth, under separate titles, talked of nothing but the merger of their families and their properties. The merged property would become Salerno, after the region of their birth; become a multi-million dollar enterprise, worked by their children and generations to follow.

As Rafe carried the tray into the sitting room, he heard again his father's voice. 'You marry Anna, Rafaele. Bruno, he and me, we work hard here. We do it for the *familgia.*' *Dom had repeated it so often, he could have been reciting the rosary*, Rafe thought with a wry smile.

But it never ceased to stir his soul, never failed to excite him. He came to love Sunny Valley, with its frontage running down to the wide, unpredictable river. Where else could he work outdoors on long, hot days under a clear blue sky? Feel the trickle of sweat down his back, breathe the clean air, taste the first sweet grapes on the vine?

At harvest time, he felt like a prince as he tied a handkerchief about his neck, and in singlet and shorts, joined the team of itinerant fruit pickers. They laughed, sang snatches from operas in boisterous unity, sweated in the hot sun as they clipped the fleshy grapes from the vines.

Dom had no need to exhort him. He'd embraced the dream, believed it was his destiny. And he was prepared to go to any lengths to unite the properties and the families.

After fate intervened and Anna and Bruno died so tragically, for a time the dream had been adrift in a sea of mourning. Yet, there had always been a second option. His father had seen it first and left him wondering why he hadn't thought of it. He held a muffin on a fork close to the fire, thinking.

'Something smells good.'

He looked up from the floor as Giorgi came through the doorway. She smiled, looked fresh, pretty, her short, dark hair damp. He thought he preferred women with long hair, but somehow he found himself admiring the way her hair framed her face, drew his attention to the fine bone structure of her cheeks. It gave her a softness, a femininity Anna had never had.

Anna had always worn her black hair tumbling about her shoulders. On special occasions she caught it up in a sophisticated knot on top of her head, with trails of curls softening the effect. She'd make a grand entrance in a revealing dress molded to her body, cut away in strategic places to reveal long legs, and a glimpse of shapely breasts. God, he'd hated it when a knot of jealousy settled in his stomach as he watched other men cast intrusive glances in her direction. Sometimes he allowed those feelings to get the better of him and he'd berate her for her obvious behavior.

The memories brought an ironic smile. She knew she dazzled him and he wanted her in his bed. She'd laugh, tease him about good Italian boys waiting until they were churched. Anna had been brittle, selfish, cold, but damned desirable.

Not for the first time, he looked at Giorgi, comparing the sisters. Despite her willfulness, her strength of character and drive to succeed, she had a beauty way beyond her older sister's glitzy outer surface, a gentleness Anna could never have claimed. Again, it moved him. If he had had a choice between the sisters, and knew what he did today . . . ? He decided not to go down that path; to settle for knowing Giorgi was very dear to him.

'I found some muffins in the fridge. Ready for one?' he asked.

'You managed the toaster?'

'We're using the fire.'

'Good thinking. You're becoming domesticated. I can't believe it.'

'I didn't have a choice. Pa's hopeless around the house. And Anna warned me not to expect her to be my slave after we married.'

'Hooray for her,' Giorgi said as she dropped to the rug, worked her knees to one side, and took the toasted muffin from his fork. 'Ouch, it's hot.' She juggled it between her fingers, and brought it to rest on the plate. Taking a knob of butter she began spreading it. Next she attacked the honey jar with her knife.

'Watch it, you'll have honey dripping from your chin if you're not very careful.' He laughed as he stabbed the fork into another muffin and held it to the fire.

'What were you thinking when I came in?' she asked, biting into the muffin. A trace of honey glistened on soft, unpainted lips.

The women pickers at the vineyard had unpainted lips, lined, dry, sometimes almost non-existent, lost on hard, often unhappy mouths. Giorgi's were full, not stridently so as were the silicon-treated lips of the Hollywood set, but in harmony with her cheek bones, and her sometimes mischievous eyes.

'Me? How do you know I was thinking anything?'

'Because Rafaele, you're always thinking something. Out with it.'

She licked honey from her fingers. It drew his eyes back to her lips. He moved aside from the fire, hot, dropping the toasted bun on a plate.

'I was thinking how nice this is. How cozy. How nice you are. You've always been my favorite person.'

'Nice? Is that the best you can do?' she jested, pouring herself a cup of coffee. 'Coffee?'

'Please.' He held out his mug. 'You're ignoring that I also mentioned you're my favorite person. I can't say anything better than that. Admit it, you feel the same about me.' She'd never said it. He'd always assumed it. Could he be wrong?

Silently, she poured steaming liquid into his mug, but her wrinkled brow told him she struggled for an answer.

Finally, taking up her mug in both hands, she said, a lilt in her voice, 'My antennae tell me you're trying to get into my good books again. You're still hoping I'll say yes.'

'Your antennae need adjusting. We're best friends. Nothing's changed.'

Suddenly, her bottom lip quivered. 'How can you say that? Everything's changed,' she said, her voice little more than a whisper.

Giorgi's eyes misted. His assertion that nothing had changed touched a cello chord in her, filled her with melancholy, a yearning for what could never be.

Taking the mug from her hands, Rafe placed it on the table. 'Come here, little dude,' he said gently.

The memories crowded in her head. She tried to choke back her tears, but she lost the struggle. Wrapping his arms around her, he urged her closer, fingered a tear from her cheek and held it up. 'Now, what's this all about, eh?'

Snuffling, fisting at her eyes, she

stopped fighting and rested her head to his broad chest. His hands ran through her hair. 'Tell me all about it.'

Her heart throbbing, her words came in short gulping grabs. 'You're wrong. For me . . . for me . . . everything . . . everything . . . is different. I haven't got a Papa. I haven't got a sister. I'm alone. When Momma died, it was bad enough, but I still had . . . '

His hand cupped her chin, turning her face up to his. 'You're not alone. Big brother Rafe is here for you. And you've forgotten, Pa thinks of you as his daughter. He needs you more than ever now. We're still a family, Giorgi-you, me and Pa Dom. Nothing can change that.'

'Pa Dom doesn't love me the way he loved Anna. You've never . . . ' Giorgi pulled back the words which teetered on her lips. *You've never loved me the way you loved Anna. You've never looked at me the way you looked at her.* But it sounded so damned pathetic, so self pitying. Wiping her eyes with the sleeve of her shirt, she dragged herself from his hold.

'You've always been the little sister I didn't have. How often do I have to tell you?' He sounded amazed.

Could he really be so insensitive; so unobservant? Or maybe he didn't have the courage to admit he guessed she hadn't wanted to be his little sister in a long, long time. She wanted to be his lover. To feel the rush of adrenaline as his body lay next to hers; to have his hands caress her with a compelling urgency; to set him alight with fire for her; to cry out his name when the moment of their meeting came. A shiver scudded through her — an orgasm of the mind.

Some joke, expecting her to settle for being his little sister or his wife of convenience.

Unable to dismiss the savage bitterness that flooded through her, she cried out, 'Why can't you get it through your head? I'm not your little sister. I'm Anna's sister!' Thrusting herself to her feet, she almost ran to the bathroom.

Alone, tears of anger — tears of loss — built inside her. Glaring into the mirror, she stared at her red eyes and damp cheeks. She pulled her shoulders back, telling herself she was pathetic and to get a grip. Splashing water over her face, she patted it dry with a towel and finger-combed her hair, tilting her chin.

Returning to the sitting room, she almost collided with Rafe in the passage. He was on his way to the kitchen with the crowded tray. 'You okay?'

'Fine.' She didn't trust herself to more.

'I'll rinse these before we go out,' he said, as if ignoring the earlier scene would make it disappear.

'Are we going out?'

'Shopping for a few home comforts for this cold house. I mentioned it earlier and you didn't object. I'm not going to listen to more excuses, no more delaying tactics.'

He was so annoyingly organized, she

almost screamed, *I'm having this mini-crisis, and you've got dirty dishes and toasters on your mind.* Again she curbed her impetuosity, and said crisply, 'Don't bother with the dishes. I'll wash them while you shower.' Whipping the tray from his hands, she stalked towards the kitchen.

'Suit yourself. But we're going shopping. OK?' he called, picking up the bag he'd dumped last night beside the hat stand. He disappeared into the bathroom.

Clattering the tray on to the sink, Giorgi dragged on rubber gloves and worked off her frustration by savagely attacking the dishes with a mop. It helped.

She thought she'd regained her composure until she heard his footsteps. Holding her breath, she refused to acknowledge his presence until the fragrance of shaving cream and soap assailed her nostrils. He stood close by — too close to ignore.

'Where do you keep the tea towel?'

Her heart quickened. 'They can drain,' she said lightly, turning to him. He wore a blue bulky-knit with a roll collar. It looked superb against his tanned complexion and ebony hair, slicked back and glistening. He'd shaved, but as always his jaw remained shadowed. A sign of strength, she used to tell herself.

'You came well prepared. Super jumper. Did Anna knit it?'

He smiled wryly. 'Did you ever see her knitting?'

Giorgi tugged off her rubber gloves, drying her hands on a towel. 'Well . . . no. But she knitted you several jumpers. She told me. I couldn't have done it. Didn't have the patience.'

'Anna was fond of taking credit where it wasn't due. She gave me the jumper for my birthday. I don't believe she mentioned knitting it.'

His casual attitude to her sister's obvious hard work puzzled Giorgi. 'Ungrateful wretch. She probably worked her butt off to finish it, and she did a fab job. I hope you made a fuss over it.'

'Oh, I made a fuss. Your sister demanded it. Last winter I wore it almost non-stop. But why are we having this pointless conversation?'

Was he mocking Anna? Rafe? Never. He adored her.

'Because you don't seem impressed. I'm the one who didn't learn to knit, much to my mother's chagrin.'

'Anna may have been able to knit, but take it from me, she didn't. It wasn't good for her latest manicure. Now stop comparing yourself to her. You and your sister were as chalk and cheese. Go get yourself into some warm clobber and we'll be on our way. Do we use my vehicle or ring for a taxi? I take it you still haven't bought a car?' He raised his brows as he leaned against the sink.

'Your juggernaut stays here. It costs an arm and a leg to park in the city. When you live this close to town you don't need a car.'

'You know what I think?'

She shrugged. 'You're going to tell me anyway.'

'You use not owning a car as an excuse for staying away from the Bend.'

Sighing, she turned away. 'Since the Vinelander train went out of service, I've always hired a car to get home. You know that. Anyway, we can walk or take a tram to the city? You choose.'

She'd already decided to humor him and go on the shopping venture. It offered respite from the unnerving closeness she felt while he stayed in her small home; from the temptation which sometimes almost overwhelmed her, to reach out to him. And, anyway, in his present mood, she didn't trust him to go shopping alone. He might decide to refurnish her entire house, just to emphasize a point.

★ ★ ★

In the small coffee shop, Rafe smiled at her. He gestured to several clothing bags on the spare chair at their table.

'Enjoy your shopping spree?'

Her lips curved. 'I can't believe I bought those dresses.'

'Thank goodness you've gotten rid of that look.'

'What look?'

'I think you girls call it a bad hair day, obviously due to my presence. I like you better when your eyes shine,' he said.

She tossed her head. 'Shining eyes, blisters on my feet, but it's been fun.'

'Giorgi, you worry me sometimes. You've never been a tightwad, so why go without such basic requirements as heating and cooking?'

'I know. I know.' She waved her hands. 'I always mean to do it. It's one of those 'I'll get around to it tomorrow' situations. Thanks for making me do it, and by the way, I appreciated your encouragement and help when I bought those two dresses.'

He laughed. 'Yeah? So how come you didn't buy the ones *I* liked?'

'Because they would have suited

Anna, not me. You reminded me I could never hope to wear the type of fashions she looked stunning in.'

Damn it. He'd blown it again. Without realizing it, he'd had Anna on his mind. Again.

He fabricated an excuse. 'They looked great on you, but I felt a bit uncomfortable in the women's department of the store. I couldn't wait to get out of there. Do you usually invite your men friends along when you're shopping for clothes?' The question about her personal life had been begging to be asked for some time. He slotted it into their conversation, and waited, wondered.

She shook her head. 'I'm not seeing anyone at the moment, and enjoying the freedom.'

As she dabbed her mouth with her napkin, her lips curved into a small arc. Today they were lightly touched by color that matched the flush of pleasure that emerged in her cheeks. He'd always gotten a kick out of her cheeky smile, but in the last few hours his eyes kept drifting to her lips. He was looking at her through different eyes, seeing her as . . . as a woman. A beautiful woman. He felt a throbbing ache in his body.

She was . . . what? Twenty two, twenty three? Had been a woman for years, only he hadn't noticed, too preoccupied by her sister, anxiously keeping pace with the sexy, teasing Anna.

'Do you mind? You're staring at me,' he heard Giorgi say.

'Sorry. So, have you ever been in love?'

She started, her eyes widening. 'I thought maybe I was. With Nathan. He's my chef. I couldn't run the place without him,' she murmured.

He guessed she'd had a painful experience. 'So what went wrong?'

'We're still friends. It just didn't happen for me.'

'And for him?' *What if this Nathan fellow had replaced him as her best friend?* The idea disturbed him.

'He's still interested.'

'Poor bugger.'

'What do you mean?'

'When love isn't returned men suffer, too, you know.'

'How would you know? You and Anna had it all.'

'Let's not talk about Anna.' He folded his napkin and changed the subject. 'I can't help noticing how grown-up you've become. Have you always worn your hair short like that?'

'I actually grew my hair for your wedding because my sister wanted her bridesmaids to have long hair. Afterwards, I tired of waiting for the two of you to go to the altar and had it cut again.'

He could feel the heat of embarrassment. Anna had canceled the wedding a number of times. He should have realized then . . .

The waiter arrived with coffee. It saved him from explaining. Actually he couldn't have explained because he didn't quite understand. But he'd gone along with his fiancée's wishes.

Their marriage was the dream. His goal. Whatever else he believed about Anna, he always believed she also felt that their future was together.

He forced himself to focus on Giorgi who, with long, well-groomed fingers, was trying to tear the top from a sugar cylinder. Without thinking, he reached for it, took it and with a quick, decisive movement broke it open, added the sweetener to her drink, then handed her a spoon. Anna always expected him to do that kind of thing for her.

'I was managing quite well, thank you.' She stirred her coffee with quick, sharp movements before putting the cup to her mouth. He dragged his gaze back to his own drink.

After a brief silence, she said over the top of her cup, 'Rafe, why didn't you and Anna get married that last time? Why didn't you get married those other times? You could have had children by now. I've never understood why *you* kept putting Anna off.'

'Did your sister say I postponed things?' He supposed Anna had to say something, blame someone. He had often wondered what excuse she gave her father. He'd had to make up reasons to satisfy his father.

'Yes. She said you were too busy, or it wasn't the right season, or you were planting vines, and then she'd wave her hand airily, as if she were trying to make light of it, and say, 'Anyway, Rafe wants me to experience life before I settle down.' The way Anna lived, I used to wonder how much more of life there was left for her to experience.' She laughed. 'You know, sometimes I even wondered if there was another . . . forgive me . . . another woman in your life.' Her eyes widened, as if she'd surprised herself by speaking of her suspicions.

It didn't trouble him that she thought him responsible for delaying the inevitable. He preferred the family not to know Anna kept changing the date, wheedling out of him, 'just a few more months of freedom.' She'd argued from the shelter of his arms, 'We've got the rest of our lives to be together.'

If only he'd known how wrong she was. A gut-wrenching pain knifed into him. He should have pressured her, but she was his weakness, and he always gave in to her, certain she'd eventually accept her destiny and marry him. Certain she loved him enough to make it work.

'Giorgi, do you mind? I'd rather not get into it now,' he said quietly.

'If there was, I mean . . . another woman . . . you shouldn't blame yourself. Most men have a lapse. I can see you're hurting. You would never have intentionally betrayed — .' She shook her head. 'That's too strong a word. You'd never have done anything to hurt Anna. No one doubted your feelings for her. We all have moments of weakness, you . . . ' He let her burble on, excusing him for something he hadn't been guilty of, until finally, laughing, she said, 'Get a life, Giorgi, and stop rabbiting on'.

'I'm touched by your faith in me. What have I done to deserve such loyalty?' He tried to smile, but it didn't quite come off.

'Well?'

'What?' He stared back at her. Did he notice a glint of mischief in her eyes?

'Tell me about the other woman. Was she a local? I wouldn't be judgmental. Sometimes it helps to talk.'

He laughed, convincingly, he hoped. Leaning across the table, he flicked her nose with his index finger. 'There are some things a guy doesn't discuss with a lady, particularly a nosey one.'

She placed her hand over his. 'I shouldn't have asked, but we've had fun together today. Somehow it feels like old times. You and me against the River Bend Mafia.'

Her blue eyes shone. She looked like the little kid he'd championed so often in the past, except that . . . well for one thing he couldn't ignore her full, sensual lips. Suddenly, he felt like a cauldron about to ignite. He dashed a hand to his forehead. It was as if a genie had worked her magic and the little kid had been transformed into a lovely woman before his eyes, which was crazy stuff. Hadn't he asked her to marry him? He knew damn well she was a woman. The difference was not what he knew, but how he'd begun to think of her.

She continued to talk. 'Only it's me listening to your problems for a change, trying to help you out. I owe you, Rafe, for all the times you were there for me when we were growing up.'

He tried to concentrate on the conversation, but her voice slipped into the background again. God knows he'd loved Anna. For as long as he could remember they were bound together; their future mapped out. Their lives interwoven like sweet-scented jasmine threading its way over a strong, dependable lattice.

And months after the fatal accident there were still moments when the pain of losing her in such an ugly and ironic happening compelled him to get away on his own to grieve and assuage the guilt. He'd backpack to a lonely spot on the river, set up camp on its sandy fringe, light a fire and drink to dull the ache. After a couple of nights he'd return to the estate and get on with life, full of remorse because he didn't feel any better and was unproductive; had wasted good daylight hours.

Yesterday his inclination had been to flee to the river, until his father's words had echoed in his mind. 'Bruno, he have the two *signorina*. Why not you marry the little Giorgina and make poor Bruno's dream happen?'

'Not to mention your own,' he'd growled.

'You have the *bambinos*, yes? Bruno's and my blood mixed together. Then we finally be real *fratello*,' Dom said, his stubby fingers scratching at his balding head. 'Then little Giorgi's Papa, he know we brothers. It all been good.'

'You're asking Giorgi to give up her

independence and return to the Bend to fulfill your's and Bruno's crazy dreams. I bet you cooked the damn idea up over too much *vino*.' The image of the two migrants plotting their future at a deal table, with a ready supply of their home-made *grappa* beside them, brought a wry smile to Rafe's lips. 'There's no way I can marry Giorgi, Pa. We're not in love.' But, the idea was new to him and soon took hold.

'She grow up, Rafaele. A donna. And you like her, yes? Me and your Momma, first we like each other. The rest, how you say, *I'amore*? That come later.'

'Sure, she's a great kid. She's achieved a lot, she's thoughtful, she's got mental toughness. She's a survivor. But love her? Love Giorgi enough to marry her?' He'd laughed. 'You're dreaming again, Pa.'

'She have the *resistente*. Your Momma, she not have it.' The old man shook his head, his eyes filled with tears. 'The hard work, it killed her too young. Ask the little Giorgina to be wife, son. She, *grazioso*, she give you the *bambinos*.'

'She's pretty all right, but that has nothing to do with having babies.'

Rafe had played that conversation — though only two nights old — over and over in his mind. And the next day, after long hours in the vineyard, found himself packing a bag for the city. It was a hell of a solution, but it beat wiping himself out with anxiety as the knowledge they could lose the two estates became depressingly clear.

As he'd driven towards Melbourne, he'd rehearsed the words he'd use when he saw Giorgi. But it had been a wasted effort. Shortly after he'd walked into the house, he'd asked her to marry him. And then he'd told her in so many words he didn't want to sleep with her. At the time he thought she'd want to hear those words, but hell, she probably thought she wasn't desirable. Heat invaded his being, told him just how desirable she'd become at the mere thought.

He could have lied and told her he loved her, pretended it was a real proposal. But such a transparent pretence wouldn't cut it with her. She, of all people, believed in the Anna/Rafe love affair. Besides, she couldn't ever think of him as anything more than a big brother.

Another thought circled through his head, a strangely unwelcome one that challenged the very idea that she would ever contemplate marrying him, even out of a sense of family loyalty. Lovely, successful, and yes, sexy — though she admitted no man in her life at the moment — she'd have a string of city men queuing to take her out.

He raked his hand through his hair. If only he hadn't made his proposal sound so crude he might feel a bit easier about hanging around. And yes, even daring to hope.

4

Giorgi drank the last of her coffee. Rafe had drifted off into another world. Time was getting on and she wanted to make a visit to her restaurant. She waved her hand in front of his face. 'Hello,' she sang quietly, careful not to attract the other diners, 'is anyone there?'

'Pardon?' he said.

'Back at River Bend treading the grapes?' She laughed.

His dark eyes glinted. 'As a matter of fact, I was.'

'Surprise. Surprise.'

'Did I tell you Pa thinks we should get married and have lots of *bambinos*?' His dark eyes sparkled teasingly.

Giorgi's heart lurched. Rafe's baby. Dear Heaven. A little boy with dark, gentle eyes, hair the color of midnight. Why wouldn't her heart pound wildly?

'It goes to prove what I've always

said. Our two old men were dreamers,'
she said crisply.

He looked at her under questioning
brows. 'I've never heard you say that
before.'

'You couldn't have been listening.
I've said it many times. They came out
here as idealistic youths, they settled on
some dry, God-forsaken bit of dirt
hundreds of miles from anywhere,
nearly killed themselves, and their
wives, in the process of turning the
earth into an oasis. And then they
demand their kids get married so they
can be brothers. And hey presto, we all
live happily ever after.'

As Giorgi spoke, her voice rose, her
frustration building. 'Dom and Bruno
were touched with madness.'

'Too much River Bend sun?' He
grinned.

'Or too much of their own wine?' She
didn't smile. She meant it.

'I didn't know you felt so strongly
about it. Anyway, you have to admit
they almost brought it off. Anna and I

were about to be married.'

'Oh? Like the last three or four times you postponed it?' She tilted her head in question. 'Sometimes I used to wonder if you'd ever get around to it.'

'We'd settled on my thirty second birthday.'

'Nobody told me.' She dabbed her mouth with her serviette, hoping he wouldn't notice her surprise.

'Anna was going to announce it the day after the . . . ' He looked down at his hands, tracing his fingers over the edge of the table cloth. 'The day after the accident.'

Giorgi dashed a strand of hair from her face. Something had just occurred to her. 'What's the date today?' Her voice was little more than a whisper.

'July twenty-fourth.'

'Oh, Rafe, it's your birthday tomorrow. And I almost forgot. You planned to get married on your birthday?' She threw out her arms. 'What can I say?' She placed one hand over his.

His eyes clouded. Giorgi could

almost feel his pain. 'Nothing. I've had time to work through it.' Then he folded her hand into his, 'Of course, there could still be a wedding.' The ache in her heart disappeared. How could he talk of marriage to Anna in one breath and marriage to her in another? Perhaps she'd misunderstood him.

'You mean you and me?' She dragged her hand from his grasp.

'You think I sound callous, but damn it, Giorgi, I'm trying to pull things together for all of us. And to get the old boys' dream back on track. You can sit there and grandly dismiss it as a touch of madness. I reckon there was, there is, a touch of magic about making your dreams come true, though. I think I want it as much as they did.'

'Maybe more.'

He tilted his head. 'More? What makes you say that?'

'Because you're willing to enter into a marriage with me. You're trying to manipulate the facts to make the dream come true. That's not how dreams happen. Besides, dreamers are losers.'

There was a touch of sadness in his smile. 'It wouldn't be a loveless marriage. I love you.'

'You're not in love with me. There's a difference.'

'Yes, but if Anna hadn't been the elder child, you and I . . . '

'Come on, Rafe, I'm not buying that line. You don't have to pretend to me. Everyone knew you were dotty about Anna.'

'If you insist. But I insist ours wouldn't be a loveless marriage. There's no one I'd rather be with. How often do I have to tell you how dear you are to me? And who knows, in time . . . '

She laughed shakily. 'I can't believe you think we could fall in love *after* we're married? That's when couples start to fall out of love. Today you'd have to be a super optimist to believe that.'

'Sweetheart, haven't you ever dreamed?'

Her heart fluttered briefly. Her life had been one long dream about him, but it was never more than that. She'd forced herself to live in the real world.

'I have my restaurant,' she said, her voice reed-thin as she prepared to tell the lie she had to. 'That's always been my dream.'

'There, you see. You have to think of dreams as goals you can make happen. They say the greatest barrier to man's achievements is his mental attitude. We could fall in love if we let ourselves. At least we'd be starting off on a very firm foundation. We're very good friends. We've always respected and understood one another, and we trust each other. Not too bad a list of credentials for two people going into marriage.'

Except the most important one's missing. A trickle of sweat ran down her spine. 'And afterwards? I thought you said Dom wants lots of *bambinos*. If we're not sleeping together . . . I'm sorry.' She displayed the palms of her hands. 'My name's not Mary. I don't have access to miracles to make that happen.'

He raised his brows, smiling briefly. 'We could come to some amicable arrangements about that. I could work up the enthusiasm if you could.'

Work up the enthusiasm? Is that how it would be if she married him? No spontaneity, no stolen moments in the middle of the day, no long, sleepy nights in his arms; arms which would always belong to Anna. Heat flushed her cheeks and traveled down her neck. She ran her index finger over the area.

'Hah, make love by appointment? Forget it. I've got better things to do with my time. And now — ' She glanced at her watch. 'Can you finish your coffee? I have to call into the restaurant.' She rose, engulfed by a feeling of claustrophobia, a need for air.

'What am I supposed to do while you're at your restaurant?'

Giorgi suspected he didn't want to accompany her, for to see it was to acknowledge that something strong and vital stood between her and River Bend.

'You choose. You can come with me, or go to the museum which is close by.'

He laughed. 'I have to decide between old fossils and your café? You call that a choice?'

'It's my restaurant, then.'

'OK. I'm quite keen to see what's so special about this place which keeps you away from home,' he replied.

She expected the response and refused to allow it to annoy her. 'You're welcome, provided there's no more talk about . . . ' She raised her brows, lowering her voice. 'About you- know-what.'

'Gotcha.'

He led the way to the exit, pausing at the desk to pay.

'I'm picking up the tab,' he said, reaching in front of her, producing a wallet of notes.

Outside, a keen wind buffeted them as they walked across to a tram stop. He took her arm.

'I've noticed you don't use plastic

cards,' she said anxious to fill the uncomfortable silence between them.

'I canceled them. They can land you in trouble.'

'Not if you handle them properly. Frankly I don't know how I'd manage without a credit card in the city.'

'You've had the training. You're not tempted to spend what isn't there. So you're a bit scatty around the house, but given the choice, I'd trust my money to you every time.'

'Rafe, I get the impression this conversation isn't about me.'

He grinned. 'Not much gets by you. I guess I'm talking about your sister.'

'Again. So what's new. She's back in the conversation.' Giorgi disliked the harsh sound of her voice, the tone of resentment. But somehow it got to her that Anna kept intruding into their day like a haunting old melody.

'I'm sorry, but you asked me, I'm telling you. She had no idea about money.'

She shrugged. 'She wasn't a saint,

although sometimes I think she had saint status in River Bend.'

'Sometimes I think you gave her saint status in your mind. I knew who she was and what she was.'

Saint or not, you loved her. Annoyed for allowing her animosity to surface, she sought to expunge it with a jest.

'No idea about money, but she had lots of ideas about one figure in particular — her own.' Then she paused, laughing quietly. 'She really worked at keeping trim. That sexy figure didn't just happen, you know, Rafe. She did it for you. No chocolates, no cakes. Her discipline amazed me.'

His eyes turned gently thoughtful. 'Really? For me?'

Giorgi ached for him, and for her own loss; for the fact that her sister would always find her way into their conversation, bringing them together, keeping them apart. There was no escape.

Even if Rafe fell in love with her, it would never be with the intensity of his feelings for Anna.

Thank goodness the tram, an old-fashioned green and yellow model, pulled in with a puff of dust and a screech of brakes, saving her the necessity of a reply. His hand under her elbow, he helped her up the high step as she struggled with her shopping bags. The vehicle had seats outside in the center of the two cabins. As Giorgi was about to sit down, the tram lurched forward as it started up, and she stumbled into Rafe's arms. Wide-eyed she looked up at him. He smiled. Her heart did a double-flip.

'I told you, you should have a little car. Tomorrow we'll go find you a run about. Waiting around for trams in this weather isn't on.' He turned up the collar of his anorak as the breeze whistled through the open section, as if to add weight to his argument.

'Tomorrow?' She looked hard at him. 'Did I hear you say tomorrow? And where are you going to sleep tonight?'

'At your place.'

'My dingy, cold, little house? Surely you wouldn't want to spend another night there?'

He grinned. 'I can tough it out if you can.'

She glanced around her. Obviously the rattle of the tram drowned out their conversation. No one would hear her say, 'If you're thinking of sleeping in my bed again, forget it.'

'It's all taken care of. When you were powdering your nose and paying for your purchases,' his glance drifted to her shopping bags, 'I spent some time in the furniture department.'

'I don't need another bed,' she almost screeched, anticipating his purchase. 'There's hardly room for the one I've got now. Rafe, if you tell me you've bought another bed, I'll cut . . . perform surgery on you.'

He indicated its size, parting his index finger and thumb. 'It's just a little one.'

She giggled, her mind off in another direction. 'I wouldn't know,' she chortled.

He joined her, smiling widely. 'I meant a little bed. One of those folding jobs. It'll be handy for my visits.'

Giorgi's amusement survived only as long as his last words. The man was slowly taking over her life. In less than twenty four hours he'd slept in her bed, chopped her wood, made her breakfast, bought her things she could do without. Insisted she have a car. He was robbing her of her hard-won independence from the close-knit River Bend Italian community, and she didn't welcome it.

Whether by design or accident, Rafe was fencing her in, shortening her options, intruding into *her* plans for *her* future.

She'd gladly have traded her lifestyle for the words, 'Darling, I love you,' but he was too honest to lie to her. And she, too astute not to recognize that his feelings for Anna still ran deep, dashing even the smallest spark of hope.

'Your visits? How often do you plan to make the five hundred mile trip? Every weekend?' And then she noticed with alarm they'd passed their stop. She jumped up. 'Come on. This is where we get off. See what you've done.' She glared at him, as the tram raced on to the next stop, where they alighted and retraced their steps over the busy pavement to her restaurant.

'More strength to my argument that you need a car. Tomorrow we buy one.'

She glared at him a second time, 'I thought you said money was tight.'

'I meant bank loans. And you know it. Pocket money for a car, I can do.'

She decided not to comment, quietly determined he wouldn't force a vehicle upon her.

'I'm looking forward to seeing your little cafe.'

'It's a restaurant.'

'Restaurant. I hope its got decent heating.' He blew on his hands before sinking them into the pockets of his jacket.

She slipped her arm through his. It felt comfortable, right. *More's the pity, but enjoy it while you can.*

Soon, she tugged on his arm to slow him down. They stopped outside a small window frontage, screened inside by lace curtains, with a name lettered in smart gold script across it. Depositing her purchases on the pavement, she flourished her arms and grinned. 'Ta Da. This is it.'

A sense of pride, of achievement, rippled through her.

'Georgina's? I like the name.'

She rustled through her wallet for keys. 'You mean I've got something right?' She smiled as she opened the door.

A small pile of letters lay on the floor. She waved him in, planning to pick up the mail once he entered. But he bent quickly, agilely, retrieving the letters, and on his way up caught her on the way down. Only a breath separated them as she dumped her shopping bags and stared at him. He opened the palm of her hand and placed the letters in it, smiling. He edged nearer. Their eyes locked, their lips almost meeting. But, as he rose slowly his mouth whispered only across her cheek.

Unnerved, disappointed, she reached for the door jamb and steadied herself back to a standing position.

'Georgina's has a nice ring, but to me you'll always be Giorgi,' he said, his gaze lingering upon her.

She switched on the lights, and glanced around, trying to forget the dark eyes trained upon her. The leather-padded chairs were stacked on the tables. Everything looked spotless, the bottles and glasses at the bar glinted in the subdued lighting. The room smelled of lemon detergent and freshness. A surge of adrenaline always shot through her when she stepped into her small, stylish little restaurant.

She'd done it single-handedly. Well that wasn't quite true. Without Rafe's encouragement, his advice, she'd never have attempted it. And now, when it suited his purposes, he expected her to abandon it and return to River Bend.

'Bet it costs an arm and a leg to eat here,' he said.

Her lips curved in amusement. 'Why don't you book a table for Friday night?' It was a mistake. She hoped he'd be back at the Bend by Friday. But he didn't pick up on it, his attention apparently drawn by a painting hanging on the left wall. As he wandered across to it, she added lightly, 'Don't expect burgers and fries on the menu.'

He responded with, 'I hope you serve lots of pasta dishes.'

By the painting, he turned on a spotlight above it, and backing off, examined the work more closely.

'River Bend,' she said, anticipating his next comment. 'I commissioned it from Jack Burgoine. What do you think?'

His eyes still on the picture, he said, deliberately, 'First class. Impressionistic, but he's captured the color, the heat, the space. It tells me something else.' He turned to her. 'You love River Bend, don't you?'

'Of course, I love my birthplace,' she began removing menus from a drawer, reluctant to discuss the matter further.

'So why have you avoided your home for so long?'

She sighed. 'Rafe, once you understood me very well. Now, you seem to have lost the ability — or maybe you refuse to acknowledge — I've moved on, broadened my horizons, as most people do.'

He approached her. 'Why did you bring me here?'

'You decided to accompany me. I came to pick up these.' She flourished the mail and the menus. 'Usually I handle them here, but while you're around, I thought I'd deal with them at home.'

'Are you sure you aren't trying to show me what you'd be giving up to marry me?'

'Not deliberately, but if that's the message you get, it's the correct one. Accept it Rafe, because I'm not giving up all this. My future is here. It's taken a lot of hard work and sleepless nights, but I enjoy the life, and I'm starting to build a clientele and a name in the business.'

He took her by the shoulders. 'Multiply your hard work and sleepless nights by hundreds, and you'll understand what it took for Dom and Bruno to get the vineyards viable. They created a heritage for us. Think of it, Giorgi.' He almost shook her, his eyes flashing fire. 'Just think about it. We could lose it all.'

'You've grown obsessive, Rafe,' she said, forcing herself from his grasp. The truth was he'd again plucked the guilty chords of her emotions, and damn it all, she didn't deserve it.

Until the accident, she'd been on the fringe of their plans for the union of the two families. As a teenager, she'd found out by default, a word here, a hint there, that pivotal to the old men's dreams was the marriage of Anna and Rafe. Her inheritance was tied into the plan, her agreement assumed.

As she grew older, she decided it would be untenable for her to live at River Bend, especially after Anna and Rafe married. So she'd gone in search of a future for herself, and ironically, found it with Rafe's encouragement.

Her eyes ranged around her restaurant. She belonged here now. She loved the hectic weekends, playing host, studying the bookings, meeting the vibrant clients, the mood music, the tiny parquetry dance floor, the popping of champagne bottles, the clinking of glasses, the shadows of candlelight, the whispers of romance.

The brilliance of feeling she'd achieved something truly worthwhile.

Had she not needed to escape the Bend because of her love for Rafe, she could have made this happen at home. Many wineries these days had their own trendy or atmospheric restaurants. But her place was now firmly in up-market Toorak Road. And though tragic circumstances had unexpectedly cast her in a key role in the destiny of the

Guardiani and Rintoli families, she had to turn it down.

'Come home with me, Giorgi. At least come home and let the idea of being Mrs. Rafe Guardiani sink in. It could work.' He waved his hands. His eyes glowed with an earnest enthusiasm. 'I don't think you've given yourself time to really think about it. I know you'd change your mind if you did. There'd be no strings attached. I swear it.' He held up one arm, his palm turned outward, his eyes appealing, 'I'd make no demands on you.'

She turned her back on him, breathing hard, tortured by his failure to understand; her powerlessness to reveal her true feelings for him. She found herself at the bar pouring a white wine, thinking how wrong his tactics were. If he'd left out the 'no strings attached', the 'no demands', he might have reached first base.

About to put the wine to her lips, she remembered she hadn't asked him if he wanted one. 'Drink?' She spoke softly, a whisper almost.

'It's too early for me.'

It was also too early for her, but he'd sent her into such a spin. 'You could have fooled me. You were into the hard stuff early this morning when you arrived at my place.'

Rafe wandered back to the painting, stilling his impatience, the urge to walk away, go wipe himself out again so he could erase the last empty months from his mind for a while. But losing wasn't something he did easily. His father, his future and, he admitted with a start, his desire to be with Giorgi demanded a cool head to continue to fight for her.

The CD player caught his attention. He pressed the starter button and music drifted through the room — 'It must have been cold there in my shadow . . . ' sang Bette Midler.

He glanced across at Giorgi who'd returned to the desk. She started as the melody drifted in the air. Her blue eyes clouded as she momentarily met his. Quickly she diverted her attention to a drawer from where he watched her take out a file and place the menus into it.

'You were content to let me shine . . . '

She plucked a note from a spike by the cash register and filed it, too. He noticed a tremble in her hands.

'And I was the one with all the glory . . . '

He'd over-played his cards. Hell, why would she want to give up this classy little place? Why would she want to marry him? She could get much better offers than his any day.

'Did you ever know that you're my hero?' Bette Midler sang on.

Anna once told him her little sister hero-worshipped him. She'd laughed as she said it. He'd been deeply touched. Now, as he observed Giorgi, erect, a solitary, appealing grown-up child, he felt that same tug on his emotions. In two strides he stood beside her.

'Care to dance, little dude?' And without waiting for a reply, he took her in his arms. The file spilled from her fingers. Its contents spread across the floor. 'Leave it,' he whispered, drawing her closer. 'Let's blank out everything for a while. Give ourselves permission to forget everything and anything but the moment.'

It should have surprised him that she didn't protest, that soon her head nuzzled into his neck and her body contoured against his, but it didn't. It felt so right; as if they had garnered this moment from the wasteland of opposite positions, to offer them hope. They stepped slowly as one to the music.

'Rafe,' she whispered. 'It's funny that song should be playing. Did you ever know that you were my . . . ?'

'Hero? Hush. No talking until the music stops.' He placed a finger over her lips. Experienced a heated longing to kiss them. Almost did. Almost . . .

Time ceased as they moved together with small intimate steps. 'You are the wind beneath my winds,' Bette Midler finished. Giorgi giggled.

He looked down at her. 'What?'

'It's a long-playing disc of romantic songs. I don't think we can go on dancing forever.' Her blue eyes laughed up at him. Her lips curved, and he knew it was an invitation. He closed his mouth over hers. Softly. But almost immediately felt her lips tighten, signaling a withdrawal of her invitation.

Aroused, needing to cool down, he opted for levity. 'That's what happens when you laugh at me,' he said with a dry mouth, half-expecting her to slap his face.

'I'll have to do it more often,' she teased, running the tip of her tongue along her lips.

Damn it, he shouldn't have turned on the CD. It had stirred sexual urges he hadn't had in ages. Urges he couldn't indulge. He put her at arm's length, away from temptation, trying to make some sense of what he'd done, how he felt. It had to be starvation at work. Starvation for a woman. Any woman? God help him Giorgi wasn't any woman. She was the most important woman in his life.

'If you've finished here, we'd better get back to the house. All the stuff we bought will be delivered after four. Unless *you* want to sleep on the sofa again. You do fit it much better than me,' he said.

Her teasing forty carat smile faded.

He gestured with his arms. 'Only fooling. Let's pick these up and get out of here.' Strolling across to the papers she'd dropped on the floor earlier, on his haunches, he gathered them together and thrust them neatly into the manila folder. As he handed them to her he couldn't help observing some of the contents of one note.

'Rather a long shopping list,' he commented, a compulsion to say something, anything.

'Vegetables for the restaurant. I like to do the shopping myself at Victoria Market.' She was already on her way to the exit.

'I'll be able to help you. Sounds like

fun. Remember when we used to go into the Bend Market on Sundays-the whole family?' He flicked off the CD player and followed her.

'I go with Nathan on Thursdays,' she snapped

'Nathan?' He raised dark brows.

'My chef.'

'Chummy, eh?'

'Convenient.'

'Give him Thursday off. I'll be around to help you.'

'He likes to check out the food for himself.' As she picked up her shopping bags by the entrance, she turned back to him. 'Can you afford to be away from the vineyard for days on end? If Pa Dom's so depressed, shouldn't you be back there checking him out?'

'While he thinks there's a chance you'll marry me, he has hope, and you know Rosa. She won't let Pa out of her sight. I gave him a call to let him know I'd arrived safely while I was waiting for you to come home last night, and I plan to call again tonight.' He threw out his arms, raising his shoulders. 'Unfortunately I won't be able to give him the news he's holding out for. But I can tell him, can't I, you're thinking about my proposal? I don't want to burst his bubble yet.'

She turned back to him. 'No you can't. Go home, Rafe. Please go home and forget about me and the damned dream.'

The ringing of the phone greeted them as they entered the house. Giorgi dropped her shopping bags in the hallway, hurrying to the sitting room and lifting the handset.

'Giorgi Rintoli speaking,' she said.

'Giorgina?' a thin, quavery voice came across the line.

'Pa Dom?' Her heart sank. He sounded so old, only a thread of life left. 'How are you?'

'Not-ta so good. I waiting for you to come home with my boy. When you come, eh, the little Georgina?'

One small sentence and he'd vividly planted in her mind a picture of an ailing old man desperately reaching out to her. She squirmed uncomfortably, feeling the weight of guilt heavy on her shoulders, in her heart. So what did she tell him?

How did she break the news gently to a man who saw her as his genie-the woman who could make the dream happen-by simply saying the word 'yes'?

'We've talked about it,' she said, groping for the right words, 'but I can't get away at the moment.' As she spoke, she sent hand-signals to Rafe to rescue her, but irritatingly, he tilted his head, raised his brows, and stayed exactly where he was.

'You come soon, before it too late. Bruno and me we wanted a *bambino*. You give that before I die. Your Pa, he will know, little Giorgina.' His voice broke. He began to cry.

The knot in her stomach tightened. Most Italians wore their hearts on their sleeves. Over the years Giorgi had learned to isolate her family's serious concerns from their frequent, emotional outpourings. She had no doubt Pa Dom was seriously distressed.

A second wave of guilt washed over her. She had to escape. 'I'll see you soon. Here's Rafe, Pa Dom. He'll tell you everything. You take care now. I love you.' Covering the voice transmitter with one hand, she held the phone towards Rafe and hissed, 'He's your father. You tell him there isn't going to be a wedding. I can't.

5

Rafe took the handset, his dark eyes glinting with hostility. Yet when he said, 'Papa,' he sounded almost cheerful. 'How are you doing? I intended to call you tonight, to let you know the progress I'm making.'

Giorgi should have walked off, ignored the conversation, but her need to know exactly what Rafe was saying to his father made her linger close to the phone; putting a match to the fire, picking up newspapers, plumping cushions.

'Yes, I'm hopeful. But there are still things to organize down here first,' she heard him say. 'It might take a few days more.'

She glared at him unable to stem the ache of annoyance from settling in her heart.

'I thought you'd be pleased. Now

look Pa, I want you to get Rosa to take you to the doctor if you're feeling so low. Tonight if necessary. I'll ring her myself if you don't do it.'

The fire spat briefly before flaring into life. Giorgi threw on a log and turned her back to it, toasting her butt, unashamedly listening, assuming Dom's end of the conversation, watching Rafe's reactions.

He still wore his anorak, accentuating the darkness of his hair, his eyes. His fingers wrapped about the handset. His were hands tanned by years of outdoor work, yet they had an elegance, a dignity in their length, in the well-kept nails. *Concentrate*, she warned herself.

'Yes. Give me a few days more. Now stop worrying, old man. You know me? I'll do what it takes to deliver the goods. I'll call you tomorrow.'

As he hung up, Giorgi sent a cushion flying in his direction. He stepped neatly to one side, but it didn't miss by much. *The goods? How dare he call her 'the goods'?* Her frustration poured out in an invective stream.

'What a damned nerve you've got, Rafe Guardiani! You're out on the street tonight, and when your fold-up bed arrives, it goes with you. I've been called a lot of things in my life, but never 'the goods'.'

He joined her by the fire, the scintilla of a smile on his lips. 'You surely didn't think I was talking about you?'

'I surely did.' She caught a gleam in his eye, then shifted her feet, uncertain. 'What else am I suppose to think?'

He placed his arm around her shoulders. 'This is me. Would I call my dearest, closest little dude 'the goods'?'

She shrugged off his arm and faced the fire, feeling its warmth reach into her cheeks. 'I wouldn't put it past you to call me anything. You're here on a mission, and I think you'll do whatever it takes to achieve it.'

'You're not being logical. I'm trying to impress you, not alienate you.'

'Then let's see how inventive you are. If I'm not the goods, what were you referring to?' She held her hands to the fire, a meaningless action, for they were already hot. She was hot all over — hot with indignation.

'A bank loan.'

She turned sharply, in time to see his shoulders shrug.

'You can't be planning to borrow more money? That's a gilt-edged invitation to be taken over,' she cried out. 'I can't believe it.'

'You're right. But Pa insists. And if it keeps the place in our name for a bit longer . . . until he . . . Well . . . ' He shrugged again. 'After that . . . '

'It's not worth the risk. You'll lose the lot. And if that happened . . . I know you too well. You couldn't survive without the properties.' She slumped into the sofa.

He looked down at her, slung off his jacket and placed his hands in the pockets of his jeans. 'You care what happens to me?'

'You know I do.'

'If I have to I can start again. Look

what you've achieved on your own. The loan is our fall-back plan. The main game is to get you back home and give you my name, all my worldly goods, as it says in the marriage vows.'

Giorgi's heart did a double take. Giorgi Guardiani. It sounded so musical, so happily alliterative. Thoughts stirred within her. Rafe's wife? Rafe's lover? Rafe's baby?

Stop torturing yourself with impossible dreams.

She shifted further into the sofa, as if shrinking from the reality that he could never love her. But, damn it all, she wasn't powerless here. She couldn't alter the reality; she could make sure she didn't succumb to the temptation to cave in to his pressure.

With renewed determination she pushed herself to the edge of the sofa, waving her arms in protest, catching his glance with a hard stare.

'You're laying a guilt trip on me, Rafe. If Pa dies, if you lose 'Sunny Valley', you'll blame me. You're all going to blame me. But what you're not going to do is wear me down. My answer is still no.'

The doorbell sounded and she surged to her feet, shoving past him, anger fuelling her energy as she flung open the door.

The courier grinned at her. 'Looks like a wedding might be coming off, eh?'

Giorgi drew in her breath. What a damned untimely remark! 'Why would you think that?' she demanded.

'All the goods you've bought, love,' said the cheerful, overweight man in the blue-monogrammed working shirt.

She ran a fiery glance over the packages cluttering her small porch. Her appraisal stopped at the folding bed wrapped in transparent plastic. She shook her head. Rafe had confessed to buying that without her knowledge, but what about the other stuff? She'd allowed him to talk her into it. To actually make their shopping expedition enjoyable? It said a lot for his powers of persuasion.

'Sign here, love.' Still grinning, the courier thrust a docket in front of her.

If only she could rewind the tape. Go back to last night, act on her first impulse and refuse her late night visitor's entry. Once Rafe walked through the door, she'd lost control of her life. And this morning there were moments when she forgot his reason for being here was to lure her into an ill-fated marriage. It had to be a warning, a harsh reminder that if she wasn't more circumspect she'd find herself back in River Bend, walking up the aisle of St. Jude's on Pa Dom's arm. Swearing, 'til death us do part', knowing the lie, cheating on everyone.

Being Anna's substitute, a cardboard cut-out of her sister. Rescuing the family. Living with their gratitude. *Gratitude? Not today. Not ever. No thank you.* Giving to the poor, a pantomime Robin Hood in high heels and tights but minus the bow and arrow, she thought in a rush of sarcasm.

Her thoughts ran on, a tangle of the real and the ridiculous.

'Excuse me, miss,' she heard the courier say, and then Rafe's footsteps at her back. His breath breezed gently across her cheek as he reached forward. 'Let me,' he said imperiously, taking the docket from the courier.

She turned on him. 'If you don't mind. This is my house.' And seizing the docket and pen from him, she scribbled a wobbly signature on the paper.

'Sure you're doing the right thing, mate.' The courier's grin was directed at Rafe.

'On your way, my friend,' he replied.

'I'm married, mate. I can tell you, you're gonna need all the good luck you can get.'

'Men!' Giorgi muttered as she swung on her heel, stalking back inside.

'Aren't you going to give me a hand with these packages?' Rafe called after her.

'They were your idea. You bring them

in and unpack them.' She sank into the sofa, uncertain what to do next. She was weary after an interrupted night on the sofa and a day's shopping; weary of the struggle to decide between her independence and her duty towards the family she loved; weary of the hopelessness of loving a man who didn't return her love.

Her eyelids drooped. The background sound of Rafe going to and from the front door faded.

★ ★ ★

'May I come in?'

Her eyes sprung open. It had grown dark and cold. It always did around five o'clock during a Melbourne winter. She shivered. Rafe stood in the doorway, the electric light from the hall creating a halo effect at the edges of his silhouette. She blinked, wondering if she was dreaming, but soon knew she wasn't when he spoke again in a teasing tone.

'You've let the fire go out, sleepy

head.' As he entered the room, she noticed he was carrying something in his arms. He put it down close to the fireplace and disappeared behind the sofa.

'For goodness sake, what are you up to now?' she asked, stretching, vaguely curious. Nothing he did in her house would really surprise her from now on.

He threw out his arms. 'And Rafe Guardiani said, let there be heat, and there was.' He returned to the fireplace, leaned against the surround and flashed a wide smile.

Like the hot air which fanned into the room, his smile warmed her. No surprises there. It had more than electricity controlling it. She eased forward on the sofa.

'Well?'

'Well what?'

There was mocking laughter in his eyes. 'Ungrateful little dude. Admit it. You're glad to have the heater.' Gently he kicked the fire grate with an elastic-sided boot. 'It beats this apology for heating by a country mile.'

'Okay, I admit it. Satisfied?'

He dropped down beside her. She told herself it didn't trouble her that he sat so close, the scent of him pervading her space, her nostrils. She forced her attention to the portable heater, told herself to act normal.

'It does a good job.'

'I've put the other one in the kitchen. But you can move it to the bedroom if you like.' He placed his arm around her shoulders.

Giorgi left it there, warning herself not to overreact.

'Look I'm sorry about earlier. I didn't mean to make you feel guilty. If you can't marry me . . . '

'You're doing it again. Every time you speak, your voice gets an edge to it. Your tone suggests I'm being unreasonable, obstinate.'

'Giorgi, don't be sensitive, sweetheart. For what it's worth I understand your reluctance to marrying me. You're beautiful. You've got style and flair. I

129

bet men are pounding on your door to take you out.'

She giggled nervously. 'Do you hear any?'

'You know what I mean. Anyway, my offer still holds. If you could see your way clear . . . You still have two days. I plan to return home on Wednesday. I can't leave Pa any longer. I'm very worried about him.'

'There you go again. I'm not a miracle worker. My presence at the Bend won't make Dom better,' she burst out. 'He's old and tired.'

'Ok, ok . . . I promise, no more talk about family or River Bend. Friends again?' His arm pressed into her shoulders, as if trying to extract the right answer from her.

'That won't ever change.' Her lips curved briefly, but her smile couldn't quite reach her eyes. If only he hadn't kissed her back at the restaurant. His touch, his closeness, reminded her of the taste of him, the acute sensual tremors the meeting of their lips aroused in her. Thank heavens he had no idea what he did to her.

'Good. Now that's out of the way, so let's get something to eat. I'm famished. Shall we go out or have take away in our cozy little room?'

'Where's your sense of romance?' She grinned. 'An open fire beats a clinical little heater every time.'

'If romance is what keeps you warm. Myself, I prefer something more practical.'

'I could do egg and bacon crepes if you're so hungry,' she said, trying to keep the quiver from her voice.

'You're not doing anything, Giorgi. Where's the nearest Chinese? I'll go out and get something.'

'Let's ring for a pizza. Then neither of us has to go out.'

★   ★   ★

Rafe stripped off his roll neck jumper. 'Phew, it's hot in here.'

They sat on the floor, the litter of the

131

pizza box, plates and paper serviettes between them, the theme music from 'The Man From Snowy River' playing in the background.

He watched her put her fingers to her lips and lick them. 'Tasty. I haven't had a pizza in ages,' she said. He pointed to the small crumb at the side of her mouth, and with a gentle smile she brushed it away. 'You could try turning the heater down, or moving away,' she suggested.

She looked relaxed, but something in her voice, in her demeanor, told him it was an act. He'd also detected a hint of wariness in her smile, the way she'd accepted the slices of pizza he handed her, carefully avoiding his touch.

However much he disliked it, she was no longer his little dude, his best girl. Giving into his carnal instincts and kissing her in the restaurant had been a giant mistake. It had shifted the goal posts, changed their relationship, and damn it all, robbed them of something which had always been special. So where did the relationship stand now? He didn't care to examine it too closely. Better to stay safely with the thought that it had changed once she moved away from River Bend, and turned her back on the tight-knit family environment of her upbringing.

He appraised her as she sprang to her feet, smoothing out the creases of her trousers around her knees.

'I'll make some tea. Earl Grey?' she asked.

'None of that fancy stuff. Ordinary tea, thanks. I'll help you.'

Placing her hands on his shoulders, she pressed into his flesh. 'Stay put. We found out last night there isn't room in my kitchen for two people, especially when one of them is your size.'

She sounded lively, but she wasn't fooling him. Her eyes, her haste to leave, reinforced his earlier instinct that she was acting. He once thought he knew Giorgi better than anyone else. Most of the time he could tell what she was thinking, how she felt. After Anna died, he expected her to turn to him, that like brother and sister they might comfort one another. Instead, she avoided him during the week she spent in River Bend for the funeral arrangements and ceremony, and afterwards slipped quietly away without saying goodbye.

During their occasional phone calls since, he had slowly come to realize that he wasn't understanding or reading her moods at all well. Tonight, her body language told him she needed to distance herself from him. It annoyed him that he didn't really understand why. At a guess, the kiss had done it. *Damn it, it happened. Sometimes these things happen. Deal with it, mate.*

He stood up and turned down the heater. Restless, he tidied up the remains of their meal, placing them on the sideboard. Next he thumbed through some magazines, but nothing engaged his attention. He strolled to the mantle shelf and picked up a framed photograph of the two families. Dom, Maria, Bruno, Valda, himself crouched in front between Anna and Giorgina. They posed in front of the sign that indicated the entrance to their adjoining properties. It read, The Red Earth, left, Sunny Valley, right.

Dom had an identical picture in his living room. He'd often wondered why his Pa kept if on show after Valda walked out on Bruno and her girls. Now he wondered the same of Giorgi. To remember the happy times, he supposed.

Running his thumb over the face of Anna, he almost cried out her name. What in hell was the matter with him? The pain still lingered, but the bitterness should have gone. He dropped back onto the floor holding the picture, stretching his legs in front of him. He rested his head on the arm of the sofa. If he could sleep . . .

'Teas up,' Giorgi said, brightly entering the sitting room with the tea tray. She stopped when she sensed the stillness, then noticed Rafe, apparently asleep.

'Please, don't go,' he muttered.

Alarmed, she dumped the tray on the coffee table and knelt at his side, stroking his forehead. 'It's all right, Rafe, I'm not going anywhere.'

His dark eyes opened slowly. 'Giorgi? It's you?' he questioned, his brow furrowed.

'I'm here. What is it, Rafe?'

Then she noticed the picture laying beside him. Dear heaven, she murmured, dragging it from him, replacing it on the mantle piece with a thud, and turning back to him.

'I must have been dreaming.' He fisted his eyes, blinking them a few times, as a small boy would. Her heart went out to him.

'You have to stop thinking about your loss. You have to get on with your life. That's what I'm trying to do.'

'You don't understand.'

She took his hand, gently stroking his long fingers. 'Of course I don't understand. Nobody does. You're not going to like this, but if you can't handle it, why don't you seek some professional help? There's no shame in that.'

He backed up onto the sofa, exercising his neck. 'Bollocks. A counselor can't help me.'

'Why do you have to be so macho? There's nothing wrong with admitting you need help.' She poured him a cup of tea, handing it to him.

'Tea and sympathy, eh? I think alcohol might have a more soothing affect.'

She sat down beside him and sipped from her mug. 'Were you dreaming about Anna?' She already knew the answer.

He turned dark, clouding eyes upon her. 'Why? Did I say anything?'

'You muttered something about not going somewhere. I thought you meant me, but when I saw the photograph . . . well . . . you were obviously referring to Anna. Where didn't you want her to go?'

He drank from his tea. She watched him through the fog of steam which curled up from the mug and thought again how vulnerable he looked; his hair ruffled, his eyes questioning. If she could fold him to her, console him. If she could trust herself and stay physically unmoved . . .

'I'm trying to remember what I was dreaming about.'

She concentrated on her drink, convinced even if he *could* recall the dream he wouldn't admit it.

'After this,' she said briskly, 'I'm calling it a day. You should, too.'

He gazed into the artificial fire. 'No dancing pictures in the electric heater. I'm starting to miss the leaping flames and crackling sounds of your little fire.'

'But at least you're warm?'

He sounded so resigned. As if the fight had been punched out of him. 'I'll set up the folding bed in here if it's okay with you?'

She preferred him decisive, teasing,

even grumpy. That Rafe she knew.

'Yes, the bedding's in my room. I'll get it for you after I finish my tea.'

They made up the bed on the divan together, he kissed her cheek when she said goodnight, and they parted. *It was meant to be.*

Though worn out, when she finally crawled into bed, her mind sprang into top gear. What did Rafe mean when he said, 'Please, don't go.' Go where? And when he went home, what would happen to the properties?

The phone shrilled into her thoughts. The handset was situated in the sitting room. Rafe would answer it, but even so she leapt out of bed, as anxiety gnawed at her stomach. At this hour it had to be an emergency.

She heard only the tail end of the conversation. 'I'll come right away,' Rafe said tightly. 'Light a candle for him, Rosa.'

As he hung up, breathless, she urged, 'What's happened?'

'It's Pa. He's had a heart attack. I

have to go. I'll call you when I get there.'

'You can't drive all that way by yourself when you're so tired,' she cried. 'You could go to sleep at the wheel.'

'I'll charter a plane. I can be there within the hour.'

'Give me ten minutes to make a few phone calls,' she said picking up the phone.

'What for?'

'I'll get Nathan to take over the restaurant for a few days.'

'Forget it.' He brushed her aside, picked up the phone and arranged the flight. She took her mobile from her purse and dialed Nathan's number. As she spoke, she dragged out an overnight bag from the linen cupboard and hurried to the bedroom to throw a few clothes into it.

She caught Rafe at the front door. 'I won't let you go alone. I'm coming with you. He's my Pa Dom, too.'

★ ★ ★

The light plane pulled to a jarring halt on the tarmac and a taxi sat on the runway of the small aerodrome. As they hurried across to it, the Sunset Country's early morning frost bit into Giorgi's cheeks and hands. She slipped one hand into the pocket of her coat, the other into Rafe's pocket, but as she sought his hand she knew she would find it chilly, fearful.

She'd left the warmth behind in the little city house that had been her shelter, her escape. Her spontaneous decision to return home with Rafe now made her face the fact that her action would become the glue which reattached her to the Bend. Her heart lurched. Pointless to have any illusions.

But as uncomfortable and uncertain as she felt, she'd made the only decision she could — the right decision.

As the taxi swept through the shadowed, empty streets of River Bend, Giorgi's apprehension increased. Rafe sat beside her, taut, straight, eerily quiet. What would they find when they reached the hospital? Fingers of fear clutched at her heart.

Clearly they were both thinking of another time. Of the night Anna and her father were brought to this very hospital after the accident; where they'd both died within minutes of being admitted.

As the taxi pulled into the hospital drive, Rafe wrenched open the door, leaving it ajar for her, then dashed to the hospital steps he took two at a time. 'Will you pay the driver?' he called to her as he went.

After the taxi driver retrieved their bags from the car boot, she stood alone on the pavement, watching the vehicle disappear into the arriving dawn, buying time, putting off the moment when she must enter the hospital.

'Giorgiana Rintoli?' a voice called from what seemed a long way off. She looked up and found a man wearing a knee-length white coat coming down the hospital steps towards her. 'Mr. Guardiani asked me to make sure you

142

were all right.' He picked up the bags. She followed him, mumbling her thanks, as they entered the hospital. Inside it was stuffy, barren, forebodingly still. She shivered as she turned to thank the man by her side, and in the light recognized him.

'Antoni. I didn't recognize . . . ' He had been on duty the night they brought Anna and Bruno in. She clutched at his arm. 'How is Pa Dom? Tell me. He hasn't . . . '

'He's resting quietly. I'll just pop these bags behind the counter and take you around to Intensive Care.'

The sound of their footsteps echoed down the long, empty corridor. They passed a work station where a group of nurses stood consulting over a report. Their quiet voices carried. Giorgi remembered that last time they talked too loudly, cutting into their grief, as if they didn't care that her father and sister had died. And she'd shouted to them to be quiet. But the shout came out as a hushed, angry sound, and didn't reach the group.

Through the glass she saw Rafe slumped in a low chair. Her eyes shifted to the once plump face, now lined, ashen against the white bed linen. Connected to a machine, to tubes. To life. Dear God, she prayed, let it be to life.

As she slowly pushed open the door, Rafe turned, attempting a smile as he rose stiffly from his vigil to come to her.

She whispered, 'How is he?'

He shrugged, displaying his hands, helpless. There were no answers. And Giorgi understood instinctively that for once he needed her to be his strength.

'He'll be all right, Rafe. We'll will it. We'll get him through this together.'

'But you'll have to leave tomorrow. It's not your struggle.'

She kissed him, first on one cold, bristled cheek and then on the other. 'I'm not going anywhere until I know Pa Dom is okay. He's very dear to me.'

A slight spark of energy glistened in Rafe's eyes. He pulled out a chair for her and said huskily. 'God it's good to have you here, sweetheart. I don't think I could do this without you.'

And it felt good in an odd, frightening way.

Giorgi tried for a reassuring smile, but didn't quite succeed.

At Pa Dom's side, she took his chilly hand, squeezed it. 'How are you, Pa? It's your little Giorgina.'

Silence. Not the slightest movement. As her eyes flashed to the monitor she held her breath. Thank heavens, he still had a tenuous hold on life.

'Don't you dare give in, old man. We're here for you. We need you. I need you to give me away. Do you hear me? Rafe and I can't have our wedding without you.'

6

She heard Rafe gasp, felt his steady appraisal. Her eyes glistening with tears, she lowered them to hide her emotional confusion. She had made her decision as quickly and as final as that. It had to be unfettered by conditions or doubts.

If she had any doubts, they were soon dispelled. At least she thought so, for Dom's eyelids fluttered.

She turned her attention totally to him, fisting the moisture from her eyes. And yes, yes, his eyelids fluttered again. His words hesitant, scratchy, he began to speak. She leaned closer.

'*Cara Mia*, you came.'

His eyes closed. She turned. Rafe stood behind her.

'Did I see a smile on his face?' he asked in a hushed tone.

'Wouldn't it be wonderful? You heard

him speak? He's going to be all right. Oh, Rafe. Thank God.'

He took her in his arms, hugging her. She felt the moisture of his tears on her cheek. Stay strong, he needs you, she appealed to her weakening resources.

'It's early days. I know it's too soon to celebrate, but it's positive, it's remarkable.' He put her gently aside and propped on the edge of the bed before taking his father's hand.

'Pa. It's me, Rafe. Didn't I promise to bring little Giorgi home?'

The old man's dry, cracked lips moved again as he forced out the words, his breathing labored. 'My son, you marry her soon, eh?'

Rafe stroked his brow. 'Not until you're well enough to come to the wedding. You're her Pa. She wants you to walk her down the aisle.'

Giorgi suspected a smile touched the old man's lips before his eyelids dropped. Fear rifled through her. 'Dear heaven, is he all right? He's not . . . ?'

'He's gone back to sleep, but he's a

fighter, he won't die, Giorgi, not now that he thinks he has something to look forward to.'

'I'll get some coffee,' she whispered, her heart beating wildly, anxious to escape the searching questions in Rafe's eyes. She hurried to the door.

Outside she leaned against the wall, sucking in air, stifling a cry. She dearly wanted Pa Dom back, and was prepared to do anything. Anything? Yes. Hadn't she committed to a marriage which to work would take a Herculean leap of faith? To do it, she had to bury the fear that suddenly her life was hurtling forward with someone else at the controls.

She didn't blame the old man, she didn't blame Rafe. Damn it all, who was there to blame? Life had a way of making you change direction at the most unexpected moments. Wiping the sweat from her forehead with a tissue and in a fog of frustration, somehow she found her way to the tearoom. As she poured two cups of black coffee

148

into plastic containers, a slight tremble in her hand caused water to spill onto the bench. Mopping it up, she reduced the level of liquid in each container, expecting more spillage from hands she couldn't properly discipline, as she made her way back to the ITC unit.

Antoni hovered over Dom, adjusting one of the tubes. Dr. Floyd stood beside Rafe. The two were in earnest conversation. She heard the doctor say, ' . . . I'm not expecting any change overnight. His condition has stabilized. You can't do any more tonight. Being here has already worked wonders.'

And Rafe's reply. 'Thank God for Giorgi. She gave him the news he's been waiting and longing for.'

They turned, looking up at her as the door closed at her back.

'Ah, Giorgi. How are you?' Dr. Floyd spoke quietly.

He didn't really want to know. She couldn't actually have told him anyway, because she didn't know herself. Except words like relieved, confused, trapped, numb, came quickly to mind and were as quickly dismissed, because now was the time for selflessness, for making the miracle last.

She managed a suggestion of a smile and waved airily. 'I've been better.'

Rafe hurried to her side and took her hands. A glimmer of light invaded his dark, troubled eyes. 'Paul says Papa is doing well. He suggests we go home and get some sleep. I want to stick around in case he wakes again. But you must go back to Sunny Valley. I'll let Rosa know you're coming and I'll ring for a taxi. Thank you, sweetheart. With all my heart, thank you.'

She should have argued with him, insisted she stay, but she had spent all her energy, all her resources in a few emotional moments; with a few binding words. She needed air, space, time to process what she'd done and how to proceed. For soon, very soon, she must be as good as her word and marry Rafe.

Dragging herself from his hold, she whispered, 'If you'll be all right.'

The Doctor looked at her closely. 'Well, I'll leave you to it. I'll check in on the old boy later. You coming, Antoni?' he said, perhaps thinking they needed privacy. As the two left, Giorgi thought how wrong Paul had got it. She wasn't ready to be alone with Rafe. She didn't have any clear answers to his questions. As the door closed her heart lurched.

'Giorgi, I . . . ' Rafe began.

'Please, not now. We'll talk tomorrow.' She retrieved her mobile from her purse and handed it to him. 'I'll wait outside for the taxi. Tell Rosa not to go to any trouble.'

Crossing to Dom's bedside. She kissed his pale, sunken cheeks and ran her hand across his brow, whispering, 'Good night, Papa. Sleep peacefully. I'll see you tomorrow.'

As she hurried from the room, she waved a hand to Rafe, but he didn't seem to notice, his mind apparently on the call to Rosa.

Dawn already lit the sky with golden and mandarin tones, promising another day of sunshine, as the taxi raced across the centre of the city towards its outskirts. Along bitumen, flanked on both sides by rows and rows of citrus orchards, were vineyards and drying racks.

After months of absence, this, the last miles of the drive home, never ceased to fill Giorgi with happiness. The thrill of finding everyone waiting for her on the long verandah of the house: the arm-waving, hugging and kissing: the incessant chatter: the celebration. But this morning, as the taxi passed through the archway over their properties and took the right worn track to Sunny Valley, she felt only a raging revolt inside.

In the distance to her left lay her home, the Rintoli holding named Red Earth. Could she steel herself to go back? She shivered. The sooner she faced the emptiness ... Her heart seemed to ice over, as if in cold storage. *Tomorrow, think about it tomorrow.*

★ ★ ★

Rosa, who worked at Happy Valley, lived on the property with her husband who was caretaker. Even the older woman's smile, the hot drink she pressed upon her, and the cheerful fire failed to warm Giorgi's heart.

After informing Rosa of the good news concerning Pa Dom, she asked to be awakened at seven, then found her way to the bedroom Rosa had prepared for her. She felt heavy, sluggish, operating on automatic as she dragged off her shoes and top clothing, then sank between the sheets.

Tomorrow she would go across to her home and sort through her sister's and Papa's things. She should have done it months ago. She'd sneaked away from River Bend as if she had something to hide. Away from her love for Rafe. She had assumed he would make sure Red Earth was properly cared for and maintained.

Until this moment she hadn't quite

understood that in leaving, she'd ran from her grief when she should have confronted it.

The minute she closed her eyes, memories flooded back, but finally weariness overwhelmed her and she fell into a fitful sleep.

* * *

Giorgi was flipping through Anna's stack of bridal magazines. She paused at a page, looking up to find her sister sitting at her dressing table applying make-up.

'Have you decided on a bridal gown yet?' she asked. Anna was already wearing a slinky white satin off-the-shoulder frock.

'There's no hurry.' She laughed.

'You're so lucky, Anna.'

She smirked. 'Aren't I just.'

'Are you and Rafe getting married tonight?'

'No, I'm having dinner with the crowd from work.' She applied a

finishing touch to her lips, plumping up her hair. 'Giorgi I told you about James Hamilton, my new boss? He arranged it.'

'Is Rafe going?'

'No. He doesn't own me . . . yet.' She turned back to Giorgi, smiling. 'I'd appreciate it if you didn't mention that to Papa.'

'And Rafe. He wouldn't be pleased.'

'He knows. He understands my need for a little freedom.'

'So why are you wearing a wedding gown? Are you marrying your boss?'

'I might.'

'If you do, can I have Rafe?'

Anna laughed. 'You? He wouldn't be interested in you. Not that way.'

★   ★   ★

Giorgi stirred at the sound of Anna's laughter, turned over and opened her eyes. The sun streaming through the window blinded her briefly. She'd been dreaming.

Rosa's bright voice announced, 'Miss Giorgi, it's seven o'clock. I wake you like you ask me.' The older, plump, smiling woman advanced into the room carrying a breakfast tray.

Sitting up, she looked around her, trying to familiarize herself with her surroundings. She remembered it as once having been Rafe's room. What if he walked in now? What if this were to be their marriage bed? The thought caught at her breath. Giorgi remembered, as an exhausted child, crawling into the big, decorative bed one night when a harvest party went on into the small hours. Later Rafe discovered her in his bed, but did not disturb her, crashing instead on the uncomfortable lounge.

The next morning he'd teased her. 'I almost didn't find you in that big bed. If you hadn't started talking . . . saying silly things.'

'What kind of silly things?' she'd asked, suspecting he'd teased her.

He'd shrugged. 'About some guy.'

'Pooh. I don't believe you. I don't talk in my sleep,' she'd said and, feeling like a rag doll, had flown out of the house, her bare feet flying over the unforgiving hard surface back to Red Earth.

'Rosa, this used to be Rafe's room. Where's he sleeping?'

'He take the room off the verandah. He say it more air.' Rosa set the breakfast tray on the bed.

Giorgi breathed a little freer. 'Papa Dom? Have you heard anything about his condition this morning?'

'Mr. Rafe, he say Papa Guardiani have good night. You wait. He come home soon and then you both go hospital after lunch. The doctors do tests this morning. Say no want family there.'

After nibbling at a slice of toast, Giorgi drank the glass of orange juice, then took a shower. Only then did she realize she'd left their overnight bags at the hospital. Climbing back into yester-day clothes, she sought Rosa, and found her in the kitchen, elbow deep in flour.

'I make you a lovely pasta dinner, eh? You drink some red wine. Enjoy yourselves. Give you the color of the tomato in your cheeks.'

She smiled to please Rosa. 'Lovely, but you mustn't go to a lot of trouble. I don't suppose you can put your hands on the keys to Red Earth? I'd like to stroll over and go through a few things.'

Rosa nodded to the board of hooks over the sink area. 'You should not go alone. Wait for Mr. Rafe.'

'I have to do this on my own, but thank you for caring.'

Retrieving the keys, she added, 'Rosa you're a gem. What would we do without you?'

Winter mornings and evenings in River Bend were crisp especially when the day promised long sunshine hours. Giorgi found a woolen jacket on the hall stand and flung it over her shoulders. It was Rafe's. She knew it immediately. Not just by its size, but by its musky scent. Her heart did a double-take. Even away from him, she felt his presence; his nearness. Here at the Bend, it was always so. Why fight it? Wasn't she going to be his wife?

A shiver scudded up her spine and she wrapped herself into the folds of his jacket, turning up the collar, then set off at a brisk pace.

Weeds grew across the rough track they'd worn through the vineyards over the years between the adjoining properties. It looked as if no one had visited her home for some time via the shortcut. But when she finally emerged into the clearing she saw, to her pleasure, the garden had been tended, the lawns cut. But nothing could hide the fact that the house looked lost, cowed by the closed blinds, the stacked outdoor furniture. Except for the caroling of a magpie family overhead, the stillness spoke of sadness.

This had been a house full of life, of lively talking, arms flaying with expression, arguing, laughing, drinking, planning, promising, dreaming, weeping.

The urge to turn and run as far and as fast as she could threatened to overwhelm her. *Hang on*, she forced herself. *Work through the pain, bury it now. If you don't you'll never have the courage to keep your promise to Pa Dom and return to live in River Bend.*

Rafe had called her reaction to the deaths of her father and sister strong, resilient. Said her youth, and being away from the memories, made it easy. But now the weariness of trying to forget settled like a yoke on her mind.

Up the verandah steps, one leaden foot after the other, a nervous thrust of the key into the lock and the door creaked open. The mustiness of the house filled her nostrils as she advanced into the dark hallway. Where were the aromas of cooking, the movements, the sounds, the color?

Placing her hands over her ears to close out the silence, she forced several deliberate paces across the polished boards to reach the main bedroom. Slowly, her heart pulsing, she looked in. The big bed had been stripped, the dressing table cleared. Somehow she had expected to find it ready for her father to climb into.

Four hesitant steps and she stood in front of the fussily decorative mahogany wardrobe. She turned the small key that sat in the lock and the door swung open. His clothes hung there, waiting. No longer for him. They waited for her to decide where they should go.

'Oh Papa,' she whispered, 'forgive me for not coming sooner, for putting off what I should have done.' She flopped onto the bed and let the tears flow.

'Giorgi,' Rafe called, entering by the open door. He found her huddled on the mattress. 'Little dude,' he said, 'you should have waited for me before attempting this.'

Taking her by the shoulders, he sat her up, lifting her chin with his index finger. He wrestled a handkerchief from his jeans and brushed the tears from her face.

'I . . . I . . . had to,' she stammered, taking the handkerchief from him and blowing her nose. 'I had to do this on my own. I needed to cry like this. It didn't happen before.'

'It was your way of coping, Giorgi. But tears don't mean you're not strong. I find they help, so don't stop because I'm here.'

'I think I'm through.'

'Can I get you a drink of water?'

Her lips curved gently. 'I was running away. But I've stopped running, though I can't guarantee not to get weepy again because I want to go through everything. It's time to make some decisions. I've put them off too long.'

'We'll do it together. But not today. We have to get back to the hospital.'

As she slipped her legs to the floor, he thought of how she looked like a lost child; wrapped in his jacket, her short, dark hair damp about her face. The stain of tears paled her cheeks, determination in her blue eyes, the large handkerchief still clutched in one hand.

He'd judged her city-toughened when she reacted so coolly to the accident, and returned, without a backward glance, to Melbourne and her life there. Everyone had thought it odd, unfeeling. He realized now that somehow she'd managed to do what no other family member with Italian blood in their veins could do — hide her grief.

'I feel deeply humbled by your strength. We were too wrapped up with our own loss to grasp you were hurting as much as anyone. Forgive me?'

She shrugged. A large tear slipped down her cheek. Impatiently she fisted it away. 'We all cope in different ways. That was mine. I guess having an Australian mother helped. My emotions don't so easily surface.'

He placed his arm about her shoulders. 'You don't have to hide it any more. If you want to cry, go right ahead. Of course, I can't promise not to join you.'

'I think I'm all cried out for now. I'd like to look in on the other rooms now that I'm here.'

Outside Anna's room, she paused, glancing up at him, her eyes questioning. 'Will this be too painful for you, Rafe?'

He shook his head. 'It's okay.'

She stepped inside, again looking up at him. 'Did you ever go through . . . through Anna's things?' she asked in a small voice. 'There must have been things, keepsakes, you'd like to have?'

'I didn't get very far.'

'You gave up?'

'I felt like an intruder.'

This time her voice rose. 'I don't understand. You were going to marry her. She wouldn't have had any secrets from you.'

'You didn't know your sister very well, did you? Anna was a very secretive person.'

He couldn't tell her what he'd found amongst her sister's personal possessions. He'd always suspected Anna didn't love him with the same intensity as he loved her. She sometimes railed against her fate, the family promise to marry him, and like a butterfly, stretched her wings and flew from him. Afterwards she'd return, lure forgiveness from him for her outbursts, declare she loved him, and they'd settle back into the scripted dream.

The dream was what mattered in the end.

She was restless, not yet ready to settle down. He'd buried the frequent thought that she may be cheating on him by working the red earth, clearing the land, planting more vines, fulfilling his destiny.

He hadn't really been surprised when he found evidence of her infidelities in this room after she died. A couple of letters lay on her dressing table. He thought they could be from creditors. She often overspent and appealed to him for help. So, prepared to settle any debts, he unfolded one. But he read only the first few lines before deciding these were not letters intended for his eyes. Nobody must know about them. He'd tossed the letters into the kitchen furnace back at Sunny Valley . . . and forced himself to forget.

Last night, as he sat by his father's bed, he could think of nothing else but Giorgi's promise to marry him. Did she mean it? Or was she saying it because it happened to be what Pa wanted to hear?

He had gone to Melbourne in search of her agreement to reinvent the dream, but she'd resisted. Now history had ordained that it be wrung from her at a time of emotional chaos. Was it fair? Was it acceptable to hold her to it? To ask her to give up her life in Melbourne, her business, her friends?

He looked at her now, fearful of raising the subject. She sat on Anna's dressing table stool, glancing at herself in the mirror. 'Gosh, what a mess I look.' Brushing hair from her forehead, she turned her attention back to him. 'Until now I haven't thought much

166

about it, but you're right. Anna kept so many things to herself. I loved her, but I didn't always understand her.' A brief smile touched her lips, 'Not like you and me.'

He stood in the doorway, leaning against the architrave, and found himself still making excuses for Anna. 'She was under a great deal of pressure. Growing up, knowing everyone expected her to marry me.' He waved his hands.

'She loved you, Rafe. That was never in question.'

'You're right. I accepted the fact that she wasn't in a hurry to get married. I wanted the house to be finished for her . . . There was a whole swag of reasons why we didn't get around to it until . . . '

'Rafe, it was to be today. I've just remembered, it's your birthday. We must have a little celebration . . . ' She stopped there, biting on her lip. 'It wouldn't be appropriate, of course it wouldn't. But, happy birthday.' She came across to him and on tip-toe, kissed his cheek.

His arms reached out to her. He held her close, feeling the warmth of her against his chest, smelling the fragrance of her in his nostrils. And gently, slowly, testing, his lips found hers. She responded with a sweetness that racked his body with an ache for more, but she had already withdrawn the invitation of soft, pink lips.

Damn it, he had to know, it had to be said. 'Giorgi, can we talk about us now? You and me?'

She nodded, her eyes clouded with apprehension. 'Not in here. It doesn't feel right in Anna's room. We'll go out on the verandah where the sun's shining.' She pushed by him and he followed her back to the front of the house.

He'd left the front door open. Sunshine filled the entrance hall, silhouetting her as she stood there looking out, accentuating the sheen of her hair, the bulky jacket she still wore. He loved her, always had. And at this moment he found her desirable, but damn it, he'd begun to confuse desire with being in love. He couldn't allow himself to take her and then ask the questions later. She was too dear to him.

Outside, he took an old cane chair from the table top, dusted it with his shirt sleeve and gestured her to sit down. She removed the jacket, hanging it over the back of the chair.

He eased himself onto the edge of the verandah, the aging boards shifting beneath his weight. How often had he and Anna sat on this very spot on warm evenings, the scent of her upping his testosterone levels.

Giorgi began. 'We should make our plans now. It would be good to have something positive to tell Pa Dom when we visit this afternoon.' She stood up, rising to sit beside him.

So she intended to go through with the marriage?

'Rafe, you're not listening. You're off somewhere else. What are you thinking?'

He was thinking how lovely she was. Perhaps there was another way out for them. 'I've been giving it a lot of thought. You don't have to marry me. There is another way.'

7

'Another way? But we promised Papa Dom. We have to go ahead with the marriage. We can't . . . ' Giorgi cried.

The apprehension in her voice touched Rafe. He felt her hand cover his as it gripped the edge of the verandah. 'Hell, no. We won't let him down,' Rafe assured. 'But we could go through a fake marriage service at his bedside. We don't actually have to be married. So long as he thinks we are, it will help his recovery.'

She pulled her hand from his, her eyes widening. 'Is this some kind of joke?'

He reached for the verandah post, needing something to hold. 'Look, it's unreasonable to expect you to marry me and sacrifice everything you've built up, for the sake of the family. I've thought about little else through the night. No one can ask that much of another person. I didn't think things through when I came barging down to Melbourne in the middle of the night.'

'Stop beating yourself up. I understood why you did it. It wasn't for any selfish motives.'

'You're so damned understanding. Why don't you tell me what you really think, how you really feel? Shout at me? Call me a selfish bastard? I deserve it. I didn't give a thought to how you might feel.' He gazed around him at the vast flat acreages of vines. 'My one thought was we mustn't lose the properties.' He punched his forehead with the palm of his hand.

'I have no intention of shouting at you and calling you a selfish bastard because it might let you off the hook and make you feel better, and . . . ' Her lips curved slightly, her eyes had a glint of mischief.

He chipped in, 'And you want me to burn slowly?' He managed a return smile. 'Believe me, I'm already doing that.'

172

'Okay, you're a bastard, but I understood your motivation. Besides, if we marry, you'd be sacrificing your freedom too, married to a woman you didn't love.'

'Hey, Giorgi, you make it sound as if you mean nothing to me. You know I love you.'

'Yes, as a sister. Not the way you loved Anna. End of story.'

And suddenly, as if a storm had been building behind a façade' of patience, she jumped down from the verandah, wrapped her arms around her body, and turned fiery eyes upon him. 'You want a good old Mafia emotional outburst? You've got it. You don't have to keep saying you love me when we both know there was only one Rintoli sister you really loved, could ever love.'

She stormed off across the lawn.

As he leapt to his feet, he wondered at her sudden anger. It was almost as if she resented his love for Anna, yet she'd never indicated it in any way before. When he caught up to her, he gripped her waist, spinning her around. 'I need an answer. What do you say to my idea? Do we get someone to pretend to marry us?'

'Your idea sucks.' She twisted from his grasp, the fire still in her eyes, and took off along the back route to the Guardiani house.

'Giorgi, you can't run away from this one.'

She stopped abruptly, swinging back, her eyes blazing. 'You certainly know how to hit below the belt.'

'Well?' He advanced towards her, this time taking small steps. Giving her a little space.

She held up one hand as if to warn him he'd come close enough. He paused.

'You're asking me to lie to Dom? Me, the person you've always encouraged to be open and honest in the past to the family?' She laughed bitterly.

'Only until he's better. It'll buy us time to decide where to go from there.'

'He's got a heart condition. He'd

have a relapse the minute he found out what we'd done. And what if the news got into the community? Secrets have a way of doing that around here. You're in Cloud Cuckoo Land if you think your idea has a hope in hell of succeeding.'

She took off again. He caught up to her, walking alongside, his hands plunged into the pockets of his jeans. 'I'm giving you a way out of a marriage you don't want. Have you got a better idea?'

'You're doing it again. Making me feel guilty. You don't want this marriage either. Be honest with yourself. But it happens to be convenient. It fits in with your plans. Do you have any idea how that makes me feel? Like a commodity, like a new harvester for the property. Bought to make life easier, more productive. Huh!'

He laughed. It was the wrong thing to do, but hell, she had a way with words.

His laugh, he thought, as he spoke again, gave his statement a sharp ring of insincerity. 'You've always been very dear to me, Giorgi. How can you think like that?'

'Easily.' She sounded breathless.

He took one of her arms, stopped her progress and swung her around to face him. He was about to demand some sanity back into the conversation, until he looked into misty blue eyes. *Irresistible misty blue eyes*. He hugged her to him. 'Giorgi, why are we carrying on like B grade movie actors? We're mates. We go back a long way. We can do better than this.'

'Darned if I know,' she whispered, her head against his shoulder.

'Truce?' He held her at arm's length. The misty blue eyes shone back at him. A small smile touched her lips.

'Truce, on one condition?'

'Name it.'

'We keep our promise to Papa Dom.'

'I didn't actually promise him you'd marry me. I had no right to do that.'

'As good as. He assumed it. And now . . . '

He caught the tinge of lightness in her voice. Surprised, he appraised her closely as she tugged away from him. Her lips curved gently.

'This time, Rafe, I'm asking *you*. Will you marry me?' She walked slowly away as if to give him time to process what she'd said.

Giorgi felt his hand on her arm, its touch, its urging that she stop. And she did, probably at least as bewildered as he, at what she'd done. Marrying Rafe Guardini had been a self-indulgent fantasy at odd, unexpected moments in her life. Magical moments when, for no reason, his image would drift into her mind. Moments when she could almost see him, reach out to his tall dark figure, feel the muscled arms as they folded about her, see the sunlit smile of response on his bronzed face, in the dark beauty of his eyes.

A sudden thought halted her. What if history had actually meant her, not Anna, to marry Rafe? If the accident was part of a preordained plan?

The spellbinding feeling that they were meant for one another invaded every fiber of her body.

And suddenly she wanted to marry him with a longing that journeyed fast and deep into her heart.

If fate has taken a hand and this marriage was destined, couldn't the strength of her love carry them through until he learned to love her?

She tossed the gratuitous idea from her mind with uneasy haste. There were no training manuals, no courses, no Bachelors of Arts majoring in falling in love. It wasn't something you learned. It happened.

'Did I hear right? Did you ask me to marry you?' He brushed at a fly circling in front of her face, bringing a touch of realism back to her crazy, mixed up mind.

Could she trust her voice? It came out, reed-thin, though she wanted so much that it sound certain. 'You heard me. And don't expect me to repeat my proposal to satisfy your ego.' She jabbed him on the arm to lend weight to her pretence at carefreeness, composure.

'Of course I'll marry you, and be proud to do it. When and where?' He kissed her first on one cheek and then the other.

She fingered one heated spot where his lips had caressed her. One day he would kiss her lips, invade her mouth with a smoldering passion. One day he would take her to bed. She must cling to that hope. Her heart fluttered, her cheeks heating, this time from a blush, though she had given up blushing years earlier.

'Why don't we talk to Dom about that? Let him make the decision. Somehow I think he'll favor a church wedding with all the trimmings. A hasty bedside service might make him think he won't get out of the hospital.'

Giorgi listened to her words with a millennium of misgivings. In the Italian community a church wedding meant a long walk down the aisle dressed as a bride, a vow to stay married to Rafe, 'as long as ye both shall live.' She squared her shoulders. She'd have a damned good try at making it happen.

'Let's get back and tell Rosa,' he said, a lilt in his voice. Taking her hand, he urged her along the pathway, until they were racing, like two lovers to share their good news.

How did you make dreams come true? She was about to find out if it was humanly possible.

* * *

Caught up in the urgency of organizing everything, apart from brief melancholy moments, Giorgi gave herself little time to regret or review her decision. She flew back to Melbourne to make alternative arrangements to staff the restaurant, to place her terrace house in the hands of a leasing agent and to say goodbye to friends. She would return to the Bend driving Rafe's off-road vehicle, which he'd left behind in the urgency to get back to Pa Dom.

Nathan agreed with disquieting enthusiasm to manage the restaurant and engage a host. It made her feel vaguely uncomfortable; as if she hadn't handled the role well. Perhaps he was glad to see the back of her.

She paid the installments on her house for six months and engaged the agent to look after it. Uncertain why she kept the place on, she persuaded herself she was too busy at the moment to cope with moving her furniture out, and putting it on the market. And finally found time to go shopping with Shelley, a special friend from university, for a bridal gown.

'So you took our advice, bought the sexy black underwear, put on the mood music and . . . ' Shelley raised her brows. 'You got your man. Well done, Giorgi.'

She laughed at the irony of her words. If only her friend knew the arrangement she had with Rafe. 'You make me sound like a US sheriff.'

Shelley laughed, too. 'Toting something far more lethal than a gun. Rafe's a lucky guy. You've got a body me and most other women would die for. And men, of course.'

'Oh, come on.' Giorgi felt heat in her face, hoped it didn't register as red blotches. 'Anyway, Italian men prefer curves, and I haven't got them.'

Shelley laughed. 'But Rafe's an Australian with Italian blood. What a combo! He's a man who'd appreciate a body like yours.'

Giorgi shared her laughter, but her mind drifted forward to the wedding night. She wondered how it would be to sleep with a man at your side who didn't love you. *Don't do this, don't torment yourself. Take one day at a time.*

On her final night at the restaurant, full of regret, she dashed a tear from her eye as she closed the door behind the last customers. As she turned slowly back, she heard shrill cries of, 'Surprise, surprise.' A group of girlfriends stood there.

They partied through the night, and

as it wound down, Shelley presented her with a small box.

'In case you've worn out the entrapment undies,' she said drawing a volley of laughter from her friends.

Giorgi opened the gift with shaky fingers. She swallowed hard as she gazed at the sexy underwear. What would they think if they knew she and Rafe hadn't made love? Weren't likely to?

'It's beautiful.' She lifted the negligee from its tissue paper, her fingers gliding over the soft, satin material with a longing, an ache in her heart. But with an effort, she rescued herself from her malaise, adding, 'How did you know it's just what I needed?'

The two days sped by, and finally with everything finalized, she locked the door on her terrace, stood back, sighed. Was this part of her life really over? She picked a sprig of rosemary from the garden and tucked it into the lapel of her jacket. Her life here had been happy, affirming. If she had to, she could always return.

It began to rain as she packed the last of her things into Rafe's vehicle. One was the package which contained the filmy black nightgown and negligee.

The larger cardboard box held her wedding gown. As she ran it to the car covered with a towel, she talked-up her decision. She would have only one shot at being a bride. Why not look her very best, make Rafe take notice? Make it a day to remember. What an ironic thought.

It was destined to be a day she could never erase from her memory.

As she turned the key in the ignition and slowly steered the vehicle into the early morning traffic, a sense of relief that she was finally on her way swept over her. She yawned, tired after the late night surprise party, and reminded herself she'd have to be careful tackling the long drive ahead, on the slippery, wet roads.

It had been a waste of time trying to sleep after she'd arrived home last night. Her mind had spun, her body insisting on doing things, operating on adrenaline. She decided not to push the journey home, but to stop and rest for an hour at lunch time, and later when necessary. As she accelerated, she looked into the rearview mirror; her home, her street, gradually disappearing. They were the past.

She was on her way, but to where?

She'd only reached the arterial highway out of the city when the hands-free car mobile rang.

'You okay?' Rafe asked.

'Fine. I'm on my way.'

'I've been punishing myself all night for letting you do this on your own.'

'You didn't have a choice. We agreed you couldn't leave Dom. Besides, I've done the trip many times. I'm familiar with the route.'

'How was the party?'

'You knew?'

'Your friend Shelley called. Asked if I had any ideas for a gift for you.'

Giorgi stifled a groan. 'And did you?'

'I'm lousy at that kind of thing. What did they give you?'

'You'll have to wait.'

'Yeah? Sounds interesting. I take it it wasn't a vase or bed sheets?'

It brought a smile to her lips. 'You take it correctly.' What would he say about the sexy underwear? She wasn't going to show him, was she? No way.

'So was it good?'

'The gift or the party?'

'The party.'

'We had a blast.' She hoped her tone sounded lively, happy.

'You didn't drink too much? If anything happens to you . . . '

'Nothing will happen. Stop worrying. How is Pa?'

'He's got color in his cheeks. You should have heard him when they insisted he come home in a wheelchair. He's under strict instructions to take it easy and leave the management of the place to me.'

'And will he?'

'He won't have a choice. I'll be

waiting for you, Giorgi. We'll all be waiting for you.' The tone of his voice lifted noticeably. She heard it with a mixture of pleasure and apprehension.

In a week's time she would be Giorgina Guardiani. In name only. Damn it, don't dwell on that, she castigated herself, pressed the button of the CD, hoping music would soothe away her anxiety. But she found no escape there from her thoughts, for the theme from 'Out of Africa' filled the vehicle's cabin. In many ways the vast African plains reminded her of the Sunset Country, her birthplace, the country towards which she now drove. Rich in color and stark in beauty.

She concentrated her mind on Robert Redford, but saw instead a tall, dark man with gentle eyes, sun-warmed skin — a body muscular from hard, physical work. Pressing the CD off, she triggered the radio, locating a talk-back program, trying to settle into the political debate ranging between the presenter and a caller.

Rafe consulted his watch for the umpteenth time. He wiped sweat from his upper lip. Half past six and still no Giorgi. What if something had happened? What if there'd been an accident? How often did you have to learn the lesson? No matter how strongly she insisted, he shouldn't have agreed to her undertaking the journey on her own in his big vehicle.

He should never have let Anna drive the car the night of her accident.

He strode across to the phone and dialed her mobile number again. 'Come on Giorgi,' he urged, his fingers drumming on the bench. 'Come on sweetheart, pick up your phone.' No bloody answer. He slammed down the instrument. Thought about getting into the car and going off in search of her. Surely life couldn't be so cruel as to plunder the family a second time.

Until now he hadn't realized the depth of his feelings for her. He'd taken her for granted because she'd always been there, steady, dependable, smart, unselfish, beautiful. Beautiful? Desirable? Yes, she'd begun to spark a fire in him, a rush of need. By heaven, she had a special place in his heart. If anything happened to her . . .

Out on the verandah, he paced its worn, occasionally unsteady boards, his boots leaden like the fingers of fear which gripped his heart. Rosa wheeled Domenico out to join him.

'You been out here a long time. She here soon, son?'

'Any time now, Pa.' Don't let the old man know you're anxious, he warned himself.

'We open the Chianti when she-a get here.'

'You not-a have any alcohol, Mr. Dom.' Rosa wagged a chubby finger at him. 'What doctor say, I listen.'

Dom's chuckle, the badinage, only irritated Rafe. He had to get away. Taking the verandah steps two at a time, he strode down the path, his footfalls crushing the paving stones beneath them. *Damn it Giorgi, where the hell are you? Ring me.* And then realizing he was away from the phone, he retraced his steps and went to his jacket pocket to retrieve his mobile. Not that she was likely to ring on that, but he could keep trying to get her.

Rejoining his father on the verandah, he growled, 'It's getting cold out here for you, Pa. Take him inside, Rosa. Make him lay down. He's doing too much. I'll let you know the minute the car pulls into the property.' They departed without any fuss. Perhaps Pa was feeling anxious, too, and felt the need rest.

Rafe slumped into a chair, tapping out her number again. Up came the message, 'out of range'. He thumped down the mobile, looked to the heavens as he stood up, and began pacing again. Was that the sound of a motor?

He paused, listened again, peering into the gloom and identified the shape of the vehicle. Yes. Yes. Punching the air with one arm, he cleared the verandah in one stride and raced down the driveway.

Giorgi stopped the car and turned off the engine when she saw him running towards her. He wrenched open her side of the vehicle.

Alarmed, she insisted, her voice raised, 'What's the matter? Dom's all right, isn't he?'

'Dom's okay. You took your time,' he rasped. 'Get out. I'll drive.'

This wasn't the reception she expected. 'So what is the matter?' she snapped. 'If you want, you can get in, but I'm not getting out until I reach the house.'

His arms snaked into the cabin. Breathless, she felt herself being lifted from the car, then cradled in his arms. 'Giorgi, sweetheart, thank God you're safe,' he crooned. 'Thank God.'

Her head tucked into his neck, her body crushed to his muscled chest. She could hardly breathe, hardly think beyond the touch of him, the smell of him. A groundswell of feeling stirred within her.

But all too soon he held her at arm's length and castigated her. 'That damned car phone. I couldn't get you on it. Why didn't you check the batteries like I told you before starting the trip?'

She laughed uneasily. 'I did. I was probably traveling through a no-go area. Anyway, I'm here now, so what's the problem?'

He shook her. 'You can laugh. Do you have any idea what I was thinking? You were drinking last night . . . ' His features taut, his eyes dark and fiery, he appraised her.

'Dear heaven, Rafe. You make it sound as if I was on a drunken orgy.' And then it came to her. He was focused on 'the' accident. She touched him gently. 'I know Anna was drinking the night the car ran off the road. But she wasn't driving. Papa was, wasn't he?'

He struck his forehead with the palm

of his hand. 'You're right. As usual, I'm overreacting.'

'You're going to have to backpedal on that Italian temperament if we're to make a go of it.' She smiled.

'When it comes to your safety . . . Come here, little dude.' He urged her back into his arms, kissing her on the cheek. 'Welcome home,' he said, picking her up and setting her down in the passenger seat. 'You must be bushed.'

Striding to the driver's side of the car, he climbed in, setting the vehicle in motion. If he hoped Giorgi hadn't noticed that he ignored her question about Anna driving the car, he was wrong.

The inquest had gone ahead at River Bend without her knowledge. When it was over, Rafe phoned her, saying, 'You weren't being called, so Pa and I decided not to worry you about coming back.'

She'd breathed a sigh of relief, wondering how she would have faced it, but said, 'Thanks. You know I'd have been there if you needed me.'

'The finding was accidental death.' His voice had broken. For seconds she heard only the soft burr of an open line.

'I should have been there.' She'd cut into the silence.

'It's over now. When can we expect you for a visit?'

'Soon,' she'd said, lying. Her answer was nearly always 'soon' to that question in the ensuing months.

On the night of the accident, Giorgi had slipped away from Anna's birthday party after the speeches because she had a long trip back to Melbourne ahead of her the next day. She'd woken from a deep sleep and found two police officers standing on the doorstep. Constable Healey had informed her Dom and Rafe already knew of the tragedy. She'd asked no questions before hurrying to the hospital. Later she had assumed, and Rafe confirmed it, that her father was at the wheel of the car. Certainly Bruno would have known better than to let Anna drive, especially in the little speedster Rafe had bought her for her birthday. Afterwards Giorgi clearly remembered hearing people say Bruno shouldn't have been driving because his eyesight was poor at night.

So why should she suddenly begin to doubt her father was the driver? Something in Rafe's demeanor, in the way he avoided her question? A vague idea of looking up the local paper reports of the inquest flashed into her mind, and just as quickly, flashed out. It was over. Did it really matter who was driving? Nothing would bring them back. Besides, she was brain-dead weary after her late night and long journey, not really up to thinking with any clarity of what was happening around her.

'Did you tell me what delayed you?' Rafe asked, breaking into her thoughts.

'I stopped off a few times to eat and rest. I didn't want to take any risks after my big night out.' She attempted a smile to break the tension.

'Why didn't you at least warn me? If your mobile wasn't working, you could have stopped off at a public phone.'

'I didn't know it wasn't working.' And then, her weariness tested, she snapped. 'Look, I don't have to explain my every move to you. Not yet, anyway.' Her hand leapt to her mouth, but it was too late to seize back the words. 'I'm sorry.' She excused herself immediately. 'All I want is to get inside and go to bed.'

As they made their way up the steps to the house, he said through tight lips, 'Dom and Rosa are waiting for you in the sitting room. Are you up to it, or would you like me to put in an apology for you? You're in the guest room at the back of the house until we're married. I've had builders in renovating the main bedroom for us. They've still got some finishing touches to make.'

Giorgi's heart lurched. They hadn't discussed the delicate matter of sleeping arrangements. When he'd asked her

196

to marry him he'd said he didn't expect her to sleep with him. And yet now he talked as if they'd be sharing a bedroom. What a nerd she was. Of course they'd be sharing a bedroom. The lie that this was a real marriage had to be kept.

She wiped beads of sweat from her brow, though a frost had already started to settle with the darkness.

'I'll put my head in and say hello. Dom will expect that, but honestly, I'm dropping, so rescue me after a minute or two, please.'

'Has anyone told you lately how kind and thoughtful you are?' He squeezed her arm.

'No, not since I went back to Melbourne, and you weren't around.' She managed a smile. 'I've just remembered the wedding gown. It's in a cardboard box. Could you bring it in from the car, please? My overnight bag, too. The rest of my things can be unpacked in the morning.'

'So you bought one of those frilly

gowns?' He raised dark brows. 'Do I get to see it?'

'It's not frilly and you dare peek in the box and you're history. You'll have to wait until I'm in it.'

'Even if it was made of Hessian, I reckon you're going to be a fabulous bride.'

'I'm too tired to respond to flattery tonight. Save it for the morning.'

He turned away with a grin. 'Say hello to Pa while I'm out at the car.'

As he disappeared back to the front door, Giorgi straightened her shoulders, manufacturing a smile, and strolled into the sitting room.

She smelled the rich coffee; heard the crackle of the wood fire. And felt immediately warmed. Tiny cups were set on a silver tray. Rosa hovered over it. Papa Dom turned instantly, holding out his arms to her.

'Little Giorgina,' he rasped.

She went to his side, kneeling by his wheelchair with new found energy, and buried her head in his lap. With stubby fingers, he stroked her hair, murmuring, 'Cara mia, cara mia'. His tears dampened the side of her cheek.

And joy filled her heart. She had come home.

'You make-a me good. I walk you up the aisle. You see tomorrow, we how you say it, we do the dressing up without the wheelchair.'

'Wheelchair or not, Papa Dom, next Saturday we'll travel the aisle together.' She stood up. 'And now, if I don't get to bed I'll be in no condition to do anything tomorrow.'

'First you have the coffee,' Rosa said, clattering the cups.

'Really I couldn't.'

'I bring to your room, once you get into bed.'

Years of experience had taught her how pointless it was to argue with the senior members of the household. Mostly they listened with their hearts, not their heads. She was about to agree when Rafe interrupted.

He stood at the door, laden. 'Ahem!

Your boxes, *Signorina*. Do you want them in your room? I brought them both in. I wasn't sure which one you meant.'

Giorgi looked up just as he set her bag down, causing the smaller box to slide from the top of the larger one. The lid fell open and its contents scattered over the floor. The gift from her friends, the filmy black underwear, lay strewn at Rafe's feet.

8

'Damnation,' he growled, fixing her with a hard stare.

Dear heaven! She turned to hear Papa Dom laughing. Heat scorched into her cheeks.

'You got-a yourself a real *signorina*, son. The *bambinos* they come quick, eh?' His wiry eyebrows raised, a mischievous smile creeping into his watery blue eyes.

Transfixed, she watched Rafe, on his haunches, gathering the frothy garments together in a flash and stuffing them back into the box. Then, unable to stall a nervous giggle, she followed him from the room calling, 'No coffee, thanks, Rosa.'

Ahead of her, Rafe's footsteps echoed down the hall. What was he thinking? That she'd bought the underwear for him? To trap him? Her stomach knotted.

He turned into the small guest room and switched on the light. Not until he'd placed the boxes on the bed did he face her.

'The night wear was a wedding gift from my girlfriends. I wasn't going to tell you until tomorrow,' she said brightly, tilting her chin, determined he should not know how vigorously her heart pulsed.

'Sexy stuff.' His dark brows winged.

'I thought you might wonder.' She wished she hadn't mentioned it. She began to unpack her wedding gown, to keep busy, but quickly decided that, too, would be better left undone in his presence.

'About what?'

'Forget it. I'm going to crawl into bed. Would you mind making sure Rosa heard me? I don't want any coffee?' And moving the boxes onto a chair, she folded down the bed, slipped off her shoes and jacket.

Rafe didn't take the hint. He remained there silent, observing. Getting to her.

Her fingers on the buttons of her blouse, she stared back at him, challenging him, when still he didn't leave. 'Are you waiting for anything in particular?'

'Don't I get to see the wedding dress?'

'I already said on the wedding day, not before. I'm too tired to be teased tonight. Sorry.' She pointed to the door. 'Goodnight, Rafe.' Relieved, when he turned away, she asked, 'Would you mind closing the door?'

'Er . . . about the racy underwear?' She could hear the grin in his voice, but refused to meet his eyes, though he was clearly teasing her.

'What about it?'

'Do I have to wait to see that on the wedding day, too?'

Now she looked up, praying for a smart answer, hoping he couldn't hear the beat of her heart. He had his hand poised on the door knob. She laughed unconvincingly. 'Keep an eye on the clothes hoist if you're desperate for a peek. Now would you mind cutting Rosa off at the pass? I couldn't drink even a sip of her coffee tonight.'

Moving to the door, she pushed him out and closed it, shutting off his laughter. She considered locking it, and then asked herself who she was kidding. There was no way he'd want to steal into her bedroom, into her bed in the depth of the night. No way. That kind of thing only happened in books. Besides, the underwear talk was nothing more than a big tease. It wouldn't even have given him a brief heated surge in the groin. Her heart hurtled down into her bare feet with disappointment, and reaffirmed the mockery of the vows they were to take next Saturday.

She shivered, and removing her shirt and pants, slipped between the sheets, hoping sleep would rescue her from her thoughts.

⋆ ⋆ ⋆

Everything had moved so fast after Giorgi made the snap decision to marry Rafe. And though she tried to avoid it, her mind constantly lingered on how she would get through their first night together. It hijacked her thoughts; so much she dealt with most of the other practical tasks in preparing for her marriage with cool economy.

Days later, with the renovations on the bedroom she and Rafe would share finished, Rafe suggested, after breakfast, that she give them her stamp of approval.

But when they approached the room, she was overcome by heat and discomfort; and did no more than glance into it when he opened the door. 'It's fine.'

'You haven't seen it properly.' He walked across to the bed, flopped onto it and bounced up and down like a big kid, grinning. 'Will this be comfortable enough for the senora-to-be? It's as big as the one you had, isn't it?'

She stared at it, her eyes threatening

to widen alarmingly. 'It's excellent,' she muttered, backing quickly away. 'I'll move my things in in the morning,'

'I'm overwhelmed by your enthusiasm.' He smiled, rising from the bed.

She fingered a strand of hair back from her face. 'Really, it's all very nice. I see Rosa's hand in the bed linen.'

'You don-na like it; it got-a too many frills and a flounches, yes?' He mimicked Rosa's voice well, bringing a smile to her lips.

'No, no. Don't misunderstand me. There's nothing wrong with it. If I want to, I can reorganize things a bit later. Let's not get into a tizz about it now.'

'I should have consulted you, but you were in Melbourne and . . . well you know our Rosa . . . so keen to be helpful and do everything she can. As soon as Pa is well enough to be on his own, we'll move to your house. In the meantime, you can have the place done up. You'd like that wouldn't you?' He'd squeezed her hand.

Apprehension tightened her stomach

muscles. There were too many memories at Red Earth.

'Actually I was thinking of putting Mario and his wife into it. That's if you're happy for him to keep managing my vineyard. His little family is growing. They could use a bigger house, and to be honest, I'd like us to build a new home sometime. I think I'd enjoy planning and furnishing it. A house that is wholly ours.'

He laughed. 'In an Italian community? You've inherited a lot from your Australian mother if you think that's possible. Nothing is wholly ours up here. But your wish is my command, Giorgi. We build a new house.' He bowed with a flourish, a wide grin on his face. 'First thing after the wedding we'll get Red Earth cleared out for Mario, and you can start on your plans.'

'I'd like us to do the planning together.'

'I'm happy to leave that kind of thing to you. Anna didn't like me . . . ' He held up his hand. Obviously regretting what he'd said, he raised his brows. 'I've done it again. Sorry. Not the right time to talk about Anna, eh?'

'It's okay, Rafe. But you have to understand my expectations of you are different from hers. And we can't avoid talking about her. After all, she was a major part of our lives. It would be unnatural to clam up every time her name comes to our lips,' Giorgi chipped in, trying to deal sensibly with the problem, though her heart raced with unresolved tension.

'You're right,' he said quickly, turning away. 'I'll leave you to the wedding plans while I get on with what I'm best at.'

After he left, she closed the door on their bedroom and tried to forget it as, for most of the day, she moved restlessly around the property. Apart from offering some ideas, and uttering general nods and utterances of approval when consulted, she in fact had little to do with her wedding arrangements. The local Italian women had embraced the task with evangelical fervor; ordering the flowers, the cake, decorating the church, catering for the reception.

Out on a flat, grassy clearing adjoining Sunny Valley's house, she found the men erecting a marquee. Amused, she listened to the babble of instructions and watched the waving of arms. Though everyone seemed to be giving orders, she felt confident they would get it right in the end. She wandered off to the banks of the river where she had gone so often in the past when uncertain or troubled. She sank onto its sandy shoreline, her back propped against a huge redgum.

She didn't resent the assumption the community made that it was their wedding, too, and their duty to organize things. Nor did she think of it as an intrusion. It was the River Bend way. But on the downside, it left her vulnerable to her troubled thoughts. As she traced her initials in the sand with a thin piece of stick, an urge to visit the graves of her Papa and Anna, to talk to them and reassure her father that his dream would still come true, had her leaping to her feet, setting off. But she flopped back on to the sand. Pa would already know and understand that she was doing it for the family.

As for Anna? Would *she* understand that Giorgi had taken her place in the old men's dream because she loved them all dearly, or would she resent her?

As they'd grown up, Giorgi sensed more and more they were growing apart. Gradually they stopped sharing their innermost thoughts and feelings. Once she had asked Anna if she and Rafe had made love yet. It was the kind of question she could once have asked and expected a reply. But no longer. Anna had laughed harshly. 'Aren't you the nosey one. Are you making love with anyone yet?'

Giorgi had strolled off trying to push away the feeling that Anna resented her, yet the thought remained that her career and the opportunity it offered for her to escape the close Bend community did rankle with her sister.

Perhaps Anna didn't want to marry Rafe? Perhaps she felt ambushed into it?

She made the connection in her mind immediately. She had been ambushed into that identical scenario. But at least Rafe had loved Anna, worshipped her. She would not have had to sleep in a loveless bed.

Think positive, she warned herself. *You have that sexy underwear.* She smiled gently. Give the marriage six months. By then the legal documents for the merger of the two vineyards should be finalized. If Rafe doesn't want you by then, if you judge there's no chance of a real marriage, you can hand over your shareholding in the business to the family and start spending weekends in the city. You always have the excuse that you're needed at the restaurant. After an acceptable time, you could amicably end the relationship and return permanently to Melbourne to resume your old life.

She imagined the community throwing up its collected hands, shaking their heads and labeling her her mother's daughter; a quitter with a soft city gut who lacked the toughness to cut it in the Sunset Country. But in the end it would be a one-week wonder. Rafe would have the property and Pa Dom would be strong enough to accept the situation.

The second part of the dream (the part which united their bloodlines and produced babies) would forever remain just that — a dream.

She didn't mean Dom wouldn't get grandchildren. Rafe would be free to marry again. She'd free her husband . . . her thoughts faltered there. Tomorrow she would officially call him husband . . .

The stick fractured in her hand. She tossed it off, brought her knees up, circling her arms about them, hugging them to her. He would father children but not with her. With another woman — one he loved.

He would fall in love again.

People did. Even her? She couldn't imagine it.

★   ★   ★

For Giorgi the days had run out. She lifted her bridal gown from the hanger, tracing her fingers over the beautifully scalloped neckline embroidered with a single row of seed pearls.

By her side, her matron-of-honour, Mary, chatted like an anxious wattle bird over a nest of chicks. 'Giorgi, I love your short hair-do. You look so sophisticated. Is mine all right? The circle of rosebuds will sit beautifully on your head. Golly, when I heard you and Rafe were going to get married, I thought what a lucky bloke to get a second . . . '

Giorgi cut in, stemming the trend of the conversation. 'You look stunning, Mary. Vivid pink suits you. Thanks for being here today. I need a cool head.'

Mary was anything but a cool head,

and vivid pink wasn't the color Giorgi would have chosen for her attendant's dress. She preferred things to be understated. But this was an Italian wedding with all the bells and whistles, and why would she deny the River Bend community their festival? Besides, what she'd just said, reminded her that if anyone needed a cool head today, it was her.

'The moment of truth.' She smiled as she handed Mary her toweling robe and stepped into the elegant ivory satin gown with its flowing skirt. She gently eased it up her body to sit low on her shoulders, revealing an ever-so-subtle glimpse of her breasts.

Almost afraid to look in the mirror, for she suspected she might see someone other than her real self, she asked, 'Mary, do I look all right?'

Dragging the long free-standing mirror across, Mary set it in place and threw up her arms. 'See for yourself. You look beautiful. You've got so much style, Giorgi.'

Slowly Giorgi looked at her image; was she really a bride? Rafe's bride?

She stared back at herself, straightening the already perfect-sitting satin over her hips. Her thoughts ran free. She'd go after Rafe gradually. For most of her life, when she'd wanted things badly enough, she'd gone after them. Rafe Guardini had taught her that. And now that he was available, she'd have a damn good shot at winning him. One night she might bring on the sexy black underwear. She even managed a smile.

Today when she took her vows, she'd mean them.

'You need something at your neckline.' Mary regained her attention.

'I'm wearing this gold cross. It was Pa's gift to Mama on their wedding day, but she gave it to Anna before she left.' Giorgi held up the chain, wondering if Anna had lived would she have worn it on her wedding day. 'I know Pa would have wanted me to wear it. Can you fasten it for me, please?'

No negative thoughts. With the cross

secured around her bare neck, she lifted her gown at the side and strolled across to the window. There she raised the curtain and gazed out.

'There's an old saying, 'Happy the bride the sun shines on', she said. 'And just look at those dark clouds rolling in, Mary.'

Mary joined her at the window. 'Do you believe in that kind of thing?'

She shrugged. 'Of course not.'

'It's funny, though . . . do you remember when we were kids, that day when we made Rafe take us out to help pick the grapes?'

Giorgi turned to Mary, alarmed. She remembered very well.

'And you told me you loved Rafe and one day you'd marry him. You know I laughed because Anna already had him in her sights. I thought it was a big joke. Isn't it odd how it's come true?'

Odd? Giorgi almost cried out, but a knock came to the door and distracted Mary, who hurried to open it.

'*Signor* Dom is here. It's time to go,

Giorgi,' she announced.

Retrieving her huge bouquet of white and deep pink roses from the dressing table, Giorgi greeted Papa Dom. He looked pale, his breathing coming in quick spurts. 'You look-a *bellissimo*,' she told him, adjusting his bow tie, reassuring him everything was in order, as if she were the one with all the strength and resolve. Thank goodness people didn't know her insides felt like marshmallow and her legs a watery jelly.

She kissed his sallow cheeks and squeezed his podgy arm when tears filled his eyes. If only Italians weren't so emotional. 'Papa, please. This is a happy occasion. We can let it all out later. We might even collect the water to replenish the irrigation channels,' she said, trying to smile through misty eyes. Any tears now and her make-up would be ruined.

'I cry from the happiness.'

'I know you do.'

They traveled to St. Jude's church in

a white stretch limousine, their emotions distracted by the vineyard owners and workers and their families who waved as the vehicle passed by at a regal pace. Giorgi wondered how she'd allowed herself to be conned into all these trappings, and then consoled her conscience with the certainty that resistance would have prompted a national incident.

A few light drops of rain began to fall as they hurried into the vestry. And then, on cue, as she stood in the church entrance, the organ burst into the wedding march. The music rose high into the rafters, filling every cranny of the old building. Giorgi stole a glance down the aisle to the altar. Dear heaven would her legs carry her the distance?

Rafe's dark, handsome appearance was accentuated by the dinner jacket he wore; his height by Joe, his best man, who stood alongside him. He appeared to be a million miles from her, unattainable, but his smile reached her, tugging at her heartstrings.

As she began the long, slow walk on Dom's shaky arm behind Mary, Mary's two small daughters sprinkled rose petals before them. Giorgi tried to concentrate on the congregation, to offer them a confident smile, but inside her thoughts leapt around like a jackhammer on hard rock.

When the priest asks if anyone has any reason why they should not be joined in matrimony, what if someone shouted, *they don't love each other? This is a marriage of convenience, old men's pipedreams.* What if someone cried out, *it won't be consummated? Or, it isn't fair. Anna should be the bride?*

Tilting back her shoulders, she consoled herself. In public, she and Rafe had deliberately set about convincing people they were in love in the days leading up to the marriage. They held hands, walked with their arms entwined around one another, stole the occasional kiss when eyes were directed their way. Besides there would always be the odd doubter who remembered her mother and thought the match was doomed.

At last Giorgi stood before the altar beside Rafe. Suddenly her negative thoughts were replaced by a misty kind of mirage, which she watched from the sidelines, an onlooker. Someone else in the white bridal gown stood next to Rafe, and yet it was her voice which whispered the responses, took the marriage vows.

'And now the groom may kiss the bride,' the priest said, bringing her back to reality. Rafe lifted her veil, captured her lips to his, and everyone clapped. The knot in her stomach twisted. They were man and wife. The ink as good as dry on the agreement. A marriage without true love.

Somewhere in history it would be called a marriage of convenience.

But she knew what she'd done, and she'd accept the consequences.

She smiled up at him. He looked back at her, his dark eyes clouded. He probably felt as apprehensive as she. It offered her strength, and as the music swelled, she took his arm and murmured, 'It's okay, Rafe.' They progressed down the aisle, interrupted at every pew by damp kisses, handshakes, and raised, excited voices.

Outside the dark clouds had lifted. The sun shone upon them. Mary lifted her eyes to the sky. 'A good omen.'

Giorgi smiled. The sun continued to shine as they dodged the rice and posed for the photographers. What more could she ask of a wedding day which she knew was never going to be perfect? She comforted herself with the thought that now the formalities were over. She could relax and enjoy herself, enter into the spirit of the festival, party on to the small hours, and retire exhausted, expecting nothing from the man who would lay beside her on her wedding night.

A shiver scudded up her spine.

'Come on, Rafe.' She laughed shakily. 'The limo is waiting to take us to the reception.'

He accepted her hand, and together they hurried across the lawns of the church to the car, smiling.

★ ★ ★

The wedding reception showed no signs of winding down, but Giorgi and Rafe decided to leave the guests to it and walk back to Happy Valley.

They were allowed to go only after a great deal of kissing and teasing and sly digs about a warm bed and not getting up tomorrow. Giorgi expected it, and yet when it came, she found it hard to quell the rush of heat into her neck and cheeks, hard to laugh with everyone.

But soon they were walking across the lawn lit by fairylights, their shadows preceding them.

'If we'd caught the tears that flowed today, we'd have the irrigation channels in flood.' Rafe laughed as he removed his coat and placed it over Giorgi's shoulders.

'I said as much to Pa earlier.'

'It was a great night, wasn't it?'

'You've had a little too much Chianti,' she said, trying to buoy her own spirits. She'd thought about dulling her own senses with alcohol, but decided against it. Now, she agonized, perhaps that wasn't such a good idea.

'If a bloke can't enjoy his own wedding breakfast, who can?'

'I'm glad you did.' She hoisted up the skirt of her dress to avoid soiling the hem.

'And you? Did you enjoy it?'

'Of course I did. It's a long time since I've been at a knees-up, Italian style.' She shivered in the crisp early morning air and quickened her step.

'You couldn't wipe the grin off Pa's face.'

'I'm glad Rosa took him home early. I hope he's well and truly asleep by now.'

Giorgi lowered her voice as they reached the house. 'Can I get you anything, tea, coffee, before we . . . er . . . go to our . . . er . . . room?'

'Thanks. A cup of coffee would be in order.'

The last thing Giorgi wanted was another drink, but if it delayed the moment of entry to their bedroom . . . Her immature actions mocked her. The preparation of a cup of coffee would put off the inevitable for no more than a few minutes. Ahead, she had hours of sleeping beside Rafe, knowing he didn't want her. But wasn't this the start of her journey to win his love?

She turned to him. 'On second thought, I don't think another drink is a good idea.'

He shrugged. 'Whatever.'

They reached the door to their bedroom. Someone had hung a sign on it, 'Just married. Do not disturb'. She looked at him, pretended a laugh. In the background vague sounds of partying in the marquee floated into the awkwardness which settled between them. Her heart racing, Giorgi reached for the handle, pushing open the door and walking in. Listening, hardly knowing what to expect, she heard his footsteps behind her. Had she hoped he might say goodnight at the door and disappear? She didn't know what she hoped. All her thoughts, her planning, nothing had prepared her for this moment.

'I'm sorry we couldn't get away for a few days, but with Pa's health the way it is . . . ' He propped by the open door. Perhaps he intended to leave.

'It wasn't your decision, Rafe. We agreed we should stay home.'

'Well, here we are.' His dark eyes searched hers. She dropped her glance quickly, unable to give him a response. She didn't have one which made any sense.

'Here we are,' she repeated, turning away, shrugging his jacket from her shoulders and laying it over a chair. She strolled to the dressing table and sat down, attempting to remove the gold cross from her neck.

'Let me,' he said, approaching.

'I can manage, thanks,' she said quickly.

She watched his reflection as he came across anyway. She felt as if there was no air in the room, and took a deep breath.

'Let me.'

She felt his cold hand brush her neck, she started, and then sat perfectly still for what seemed an eon.

'Can you manage?' she finally asked.

'The catch isn't meant for big hands.'

'I said I could do it.'

Their words and voices sounded formal, contrived, unnatural, like amateurs performing in a church hall. *Lighten up*, Giorgi told herself.

She held the locket in her hand and watched as he dropped onto the bed and began removing a shoe.

'Would you like to change in the dressing room first?' he asked.

'Would you mind if I took a shower? Can you wait?'

He looked up sharply from the bed where he tugged off a second shoe. 'Wait? What for?'

226

9

Giorgi almost cringed at her unfortunate phrasing. 'To use the bathroom.'

His second shoe in hand, he said, 'Gotcha. For a minute you had me going there.'

'Do you want to use the bathroom first or not?' Her voice rose sharply.

'I can use the one down the passage if I get caught short.' He stretched out across the bed and yawned.

'Don't you dare go to sleep sprawled all over the doona like that,' she warned, alarmed, remembering the last time he'd claimed her bed by falling into a deep sleep.

He must have remembered, too, for a brief smile lit his eyes. 'The quicker you have your shower, Giorgi, the quicker we can get to bed.' He put his feet to the carpet, plumped up a few pillows and lay down again, his arms stretched behind his head.

If only she felt as at ease as he looked. 'I'm going,' she said, hot one minute, cold the next.

Entering the en suite, she closed the door, noting there was no lock. But who needed a lock when the certainty was he had no intention of following her, of sharing the warm spray of water, caressing her naked body with hands . . . The heat of her thoughts stampeded into every part of her body. She reached for the edge of the shower screen and clung to it, dragging in air. She had nobody to blame but herself for the dilemma in which she found herself, yet she tortured herself imagining what could have been.

'You all right in there? I can't hear the shower.'

'I've got a wedding dress to get out of.' She called back, springing into action.

'Do you need any help?'

He could help her out of her dress, and not want to touch her, hold her, kiss her. She ran the palm of her hand across her forehead, her heart in revolt. So this was her wedding night.

She put her head around the door. 'Look, Rafe, I know you were enjoying yourself. Why don't you go back to the party?'

'You have to be joking. I'm beat. I couldn't raise a gallop if they paid me.'

Was he pleading weariness as an excuse from the marriage bed? Should she be pleased or disappointed? She was certainly confused.

'You shouldn't have worked all day.'

'Anyway, what would the guests think if I left my bride on our wedding night?'

If only she could shrug and say carelessly, 'Who cares? We're playing a game'. But she did care. They had to give a convincing performance to Papa Dom, so his health would continue to improve.

Anxiously, she turned on the shower to cut off the need to reply, or for any further conversation, and unzipped her wedding gown. It dropped to the floor and she slipped out of it, retrieving and laying it over a stool. If she took long enough, Rafe might fall asleep. She might be able to get into the big bed without disturbing him. Memories of his visit to her Melbourne terrace continued to trouble and confuse her.

But when she stepped under the shower, the warm water soothed her as it coursed over her. She breathed in the fragrance of the foaming liquid soap, tracing her fingers down her legs, stretching her arms, and finally beginning to unwind and let the tension flow from her body. Whatever happened, she could deal with it.

Toweling herself dry, she traced her initials — G.R. in the steam-coated mirror over the basin, and gasped. Rafe's initials back to front. And then acknowledged her initials offically now were G.G. — Giorgina Guardini. She amended the R, playing with time, postponing her re-entry into the bedroom. Next she carried her dress to the new dressing room Rafe had added for her, and slid open the mirrored door to the robes. To her surprise, she found all her clothes hung there.

Thoughtful Rosa had apparently been at work here, too. She sat on the lounge and pulled a short, cotton nightshirt over her head. Printed on it were the region's latest tourist words, 'Visit the Sunset Country and fall in love'. Suddenly it seemed wrong. She thought of the filmy black underwear, still in its box. That too would have been wrong, too obvious. How did a bride whose husband didn't love her dress for bed on their wedding night?

You've got your integrity, your honesty intact. You've done the right thing. Your emotional stability will come.

Tilting her chin, she threw her robe over her cotton shirt, and forced herself to the bedroom door. Rafe sat up the instant she re-entered. Her nipples peaked alarmingly as his dark gaze swept over her. Thank heaven for the robe.

He slid off the bed, came to her. Her leaden feet weren't quick enough to avoid his touch as he reached out to her. 'You smell nice.'

'Nice?' she responded parrot-fashion.

He held her at arm's length. Desire ribboned through her. She searched his eyes for the heat of his arousal as he gazed upon her, but found only warmth — the big brother look she was so used to. *Damn it all, I'm your wife now. Can't you want me just a little?*

'Giorgi, thank you for today. I'll never forget what you've sacrificed for the family. If your father knew, he'd be so proud of you.' He kissed her then, one cheek at a time — the old Rafe, her friend. Anna's lover; the Rafe Giorgi understood best.

'Please,' her voice sounded spent, tired. 'Your gratitude is starting to wear rather thin. I thought this marriage was a team affair. Once your Pa's all right, we can start thinking about . . . er . . . our own futures again.'

'You're bushed.' He released her. 'Go

to bed little dude . . . oops . . . sorry, I can't help thinking of you as . . . ' Displaying his open palms as if to ward off an angry response, he added, 'Sleep tight,' before removing his tie. He began to hum as he entered the en suite.

She hurried around to the far side of the bed, climbed in and pulled the sheet and duvet up to her ears, as if to disappear. Turning her body towards the window, she closed her eyes and prayed for sleep, yet found herself mentally attuned to the slightest sounds coming from the bathroom.

All knotted up inside, she tried to psych herself up for his return; for the moment when he would lift back the sheet and she'd feel the movement of the bed as he slipped between the sheets and turned his back on her. Would he say to himself with a smile on his lips, 'mission accomplished', as he fell into a peaceful sleep? Content that today he had saved the damned dream?

★   ★   ★

The fragrance of her was everywhere in the en suite. Rafe turned on the shower, giving the cold water an extra turn. It had taken every ounce of control to walk away from Giorgi. She was his wife now, for God's sake, that gave him legal rights. *But what good were legal rights, when in your heart you knew you had no moral right to take her? When you told her you didn't expect her to sleep with you. You, poor fool, had no idea how much she'd excite you. Send your testosterone levels soaring, your need running riot.*

He rubbed vigorously at his body, as if to wipe the smell of her, the need of her from him. Okay, she wasn't the woman he was supposed to marry, but today as she walked down the aisle, as she smiled gently up at him when she arrived to stand beside him at the altar, as she promised to love him forever. God he'd felt touched, profoundly committed to her. And during the reception, he'd tried unsuccessfully to ignore the heat in his loins, his arousal as he held her close and they danced. He'd thought she didn't have Anna's sexual appeal. Damn it, she had it in triplicate.

Go back to her bed. Test her feelings, be gentle. She might be receptive.

Who the hell was he kidding? She was his in name only. They had a pact he couldn't allow his physical need to plunder. A pact he must keep at all costs if he were to live with himself.

Rubbing himself dry with hard, vicious strokes of the towel, as if to expunge his baser feelings, he walked to the dressing room where Rosa had left pillows and a duvet in one of the robes. He'd lied to the housekeeper, telling her that on the nights he sat up late poring over the property accounts, he would bed down on the divan rather than disturb Giorgi.

He threw the sheets and cover carelessly onto the divan, lied down, stretching his arms behind his head and gazing up at the ceiling. What a hell of a wedding night.

Once he and Anna had planned to honeymoon on Daydream Island. She'd talked of rollicking and carousing between the sheets, a warm ocean breeze feathering through the gossamer curtains, working him into a lather of anticipation.

In all the years they were an item, only twice had they made love. He'd been too eager, too quick. It was all over in a majestic, spine-tingling moment. The next time, it'll be different, he told himself. But it wasn't for Anna had changed the rules. She was a real tease. She'd cup his hands to her covered breasts, he'd sweep aside one shoulder of her clothing, nibble her ear, place his lips to her skin. And she'd laugh, her full-throated laugh.

'What would Pa say if he knew what you were up to?' She'd raise her salon-styled eyebrows, proffer a pouty smile. Turn him on. Small wonder men flocked around her. Small wonder he had occasional flings with other women, especially after she'd worked him up and left him hanging out to dry.

She craved attention, the admiration of men. Gradually the thought that she didn't know the meaning of faithfulness and would make a lousy wife, began to torment him in dark moments. But he couldn't abandon the million dollar dream. He had to give it his best shot and hope that Anna would settle down once they were married.

But it had all become academic. Even if she hadn't died that night, the marriage wouldn't have gone ahead.

It was well into the early morning, her birthday party on its last legs. He'd found Anna's suitcases on the back verandah of Red Earth when he went in search of her. She was leaving the Bend with another man.

Well, he'd married Giorgi. The lovely Giorgi had become his wife. He wondered again what would happen if he went to her bed. Would she let him in? To her bed, to her body. He had no right, but hell and damnation anything was better than lying here torturing himself, trying to decide.

Let her decide. If she responds in any way . . . He wound the duvet loosely around his nakedness and walked quietly through the en suite towards the bedroom.

★   ★   ★

When Giorgi heard the door open, the ever-so-slight sound of footfalls, she lay very still, her body tightly coiled, hardly breathing. Once he climbed in beside her, laying his body next to hers, would he want her?

Soon she would have to decide. Soon. If he held her, kissed her, caressed her . . . If he tried to claim her as his wife, would she resist?

A movement, a vague swishing sound and her heart jumped. She clutched at the edge of the sheet. What was going on? Was it Rafe? Summoning a dash of courage, she sat up, bringing the sheet with her.

'Is that you, Rafe?'

'Yes. Sorry, have I woken you?'

As her eyes became accustomed to the gloom, she made out his figure draped in a blanket, holding a pillow in one hand. She wondered why he appeared riveted to the carpet.

Forcing the words, she asked, 'What on earth are you doing?'

He took a step closer to the bed, reaching for a second pillow. She wriggled closer to the edge of the bed. If only she could see his eyes clearly . . . If only she knew what he was thinking . . .

'I came back for a couple of these.' He indicated the pillows.

Her mouth probably fell open. She adjusted the sheet under her chin, staring at him. 'Came back? Where were you going?'

'To the dressing room.' He sounded a little strained.

'Oh, the dressing room?' Her voice rose.

He forced the pillows under one arm, juggling the duvet around his waist.

'Didn't I mention, I'll be sleeping in there on the day-nighter? I can't go to another room, or Pa will know we're not sharing a bed.'

She swallowed. A strange alchemy of disappointment and relief swept over her. 'I wasn't sure what arrangements you'd made. I suppose I should have inquired, but I knew you'd work something out,' she said as if it wasn't in the least of interest to her. 'If I sound a bit vague, it's because you woke me. I felt disoriented for a minute. Well, if you've got enough pillows, if there's nothing else . . . Goodnight again.'

She sensed his dark gaze travel over her as she sank into the vast, empty bed. Was he asking something with his eyes?

She switched on the bedside lamp, hoping the cold light would hold back the tide of emotions washing over her.

'No.' He wrestled to hold the pillows, the duvet slipped. He dragged it back to his waist.

She'd often seen him bare-chested,

delighting in the way his muscles tensed and relaxed, his body gleaming with sweat as he'd pruned the vines in the winter sun. And loved him. Always, she had loved him, her heart cried.

Invite him into your bed. Say it. It's your wedding night. Tell him he doesn't have to sleep on a lonely divan. But her mouth felt dry, refused the words. And closing her eyes, she willed the temptation to fall away. How could she belittle her love for him by stealing a few moments of passion? And what if he discovered that she loved him? Would he feel obligated to her?

She wanted his love, not an occasional carousal in the marriage bed.

'Did I say thank you for doing this for Pa?' He rested the pillows at the foot of the bed, as if buying time, rearranging the duvet about his shoulders.

'A hundred times.' She felt edgy, confused. 'For goodness sake, you must be cold, Rafe. Go to bed. I'll see you tomorrow.'

'I'm off. See you.' As he reached for the pillows, the duvet dropped to the floor. He was naked.

'Bloody hell,' he rasped.

As he dragged the cover back over his torso, heat filled her body. Her heart went on hold. In his nakedness, in the beam of the bedside lamp, her thoughts flashed to Michelangelo's statue of David. Physical, athletic, strong. Cast in marble.

The pillows fell from his grasp. He swore, grabbing them up with his free arm and stuffing them under it.

'I bet you weren't expecting the full monty,' he said, straining; she thought, to sound lighthearted. But neither of them laughed.

'I don't know what I was expecting,' she whispered, sinking back into the bed and reaching to extinguish the light.

'See you in the morning,' she heard him say as darkness closed over the room.

As the sound of his feet drifted away,

she damned herself for the uncertainty; the insecurity that had made her behave in such an ambivalent, purposeless manner on her wedding night.

If only she were back in her city house, in control of her life and her thoughts.

10

At Sunny Valley, Giorgi managed to convince Rosa that she should have responsibility for caring for their bed-room suite. It gave her something to do, she said, but in fact the main purpose was to avoid the risk of anyone discovering she and Rafe didn't sleep together. One thing, however, they couldn't avoid were Pa Dom's almost daily inquiries.

At breakfast this morning he'd asked again, looking intently at her middle with sharp blue eyes, 'When you get the swollen belly, Giorgi? The *bambino*, it come soon?' He'd rubbed his hands, lined and dry with time and industry, together and smiled. 'Ma and me, we have Rafaele nine months after . . . '

Rafe interrupted. 'It must have been a fluke.' He laughed. 'You and Ma didn't manage any more *bambinos* after me, so don't go getting carried away.'

'But Giorgi young, strong, no hard work like your Mama.' Tears filled his eyes.

'Pa, there's no need to get upset,' Giorgi said with a touch of impatience.

'You always working son. You never here to make the *bambinos*.'

Giorgi rose, kissing his cheek. 'Babies happen in their own sweet time. We're doing our best.' She tried to curve her lips, but the curve felt more like a curl, the curl of lying lips. As she started to leave the room, she let Rafe know how frustrated she felt with a sidelong glare and by mouthing the words that she was getting very sick of Pa's carping.

'Where you going, little Giorgi?' the old man asked.

'I'm spending the day at Red Earth,' she announced, flouncing out.

Rafe caught up with her in the passageway, steering her into the lounge room and closing the door. 'We have to talk, Giorgi.'

Since that first night he hadn't come

into the bedroom, he'd referred to it as 'your bedroom'. He'd stopped touching her, looking affectionately at her with dark, gentle eyes, being her big brother. These days when his glance shifted to her, she doubted if he even saw her.

In the beginning she'd welcomed his long absences in the vineyard, the lateness of him moving around in the en suite and dressing room, but soon the emptiness of her days mocked her. She longed for her restaurant, for a project to occupy her mind and give some purpose to her existence. Anything to banish the thought that she'd become locked into a phony marriage.

Despite Pa's protests that it wasn't women's work, she insisted on taking over the books of the two vineyards. It helped her through an otherwise pointless day, but the nights remained repetitive and joyless.

Now anger bubbled up inside her. 'Of course we need to talk, but are you sure you can spare the time?' She lashed out, gripping the back of a chair.

'I've been trying not to get in your way.' Cold, dark eyes flickered over her. 'I thought that's what you wanted.'

It was, wasn't it? Her stomach turned over. She threw her arms in the air. 'Just for once, I'd like to get up in the morning and know I had something to look forward to.'

He slowly, deliberately, shoved up the sleeves of his shirt, reawakening her weakness for his strength; his tanned, muscled arms, momentarily hijacking her attention, quelling her anger.

'Tomorrow you can. We've got an appointment with the solicitors. We need to sign the papers to legally merge the two properties. Is that worthwhile enough to get you out of bed? Unless, of course, you've suddenly decided against the merger.'

His taunt refocused her. 'So why has it taken you this long to inform me?'

'Have you changed your mind then?'

'Don't be absurd. It's the reason for this ludicrous sham of a marriage.' She brushed a strand of hair from her face, hating the steeliness in her voice. 'It's the only reason.'

'You think I'm not aware of that? After tomorrow you can have out any time you like.' He laughed harshly, placing his back to the window as if to close out the morning light.

'Oh, sure. You know damned well Pa's not yet strong enough to cope with that kind of shock. His only child divorced after a few months of marriage. It could kill him.' She crashed into a chair.

He threw up his hands. 'Hell, Giorgi, what else can I say? What do you want from me?'

She closed her eyes, then looked to the ceiling. How easy to cry out, 'I want you. I want you to love me.' Instead, she said, 'I don't know.' Her voice dropped to a whisper when she repeated, 'I just don't know.'

Rafe hurried to her side, knelt by the chair and took her hands in his. 'I'm terribly sorry, little dude. You've given up so much and it's not working for you, is it?'

The sudden gentleness in his eyes, in his voice, in his touch, brought a rush of tears to her eyes. She fought them off, shaking her head, not trusting herself to speak.

'Why don't you spend a few days back in Melbourne, catch up with your friends and the restaurant? I've taken you for granted, left you to your own devices. There's not much around here for you to get stuck into, is there?' He stood up, slapping the palm of his hand against his forehead. 'God, I've been a thoughtless brute. It must be boring as hell when you're so used to running your own business, having people you relate to around you, making decisions . . . '

A shaft of sunshine penetrated her gloomy mood. A few days away from the tension of living the lie, staying cheerful and patient with Pa, and having to acknowledge that Rafe wasn't going to fall in love with her, was exactly what she needed.

'Could you cover for me? Pa might get suspicious. He won't like it.'

He gazed down at her, his eyes glinting. 'Let's think of you and your needs for once. We'll tell him you're going down to buy a layette for the baby.'

Furious, she edged forward in the chair, restraining herself from lashing out at him. 'I beg your pardon?'

His raised his shoulders. 'He wouldn't question that.'

'But I would. I can't believe you. We've lied to him enough.'

'OK. It sounds callous, but our motives have always been in his interest.'

'Yours or his?' she asked harshly.

'I'm trying to find a way out for you.'

'By telling him more lies? No thank you. I have some business matters associated with the restaurant that need my attention. I should go to Melbourne anyway. Agreed?'

'I don't see why not. Fine,' he said.

'I'll tell him tonight, and after we've seen the lawyer tomorrow, you can make your own decision about when you go, and how long you stay away.'

And without waiting for her approval, he left the room without a backward glance, giving her the distinct feeling he'd welcome her absence. And it occurred to her that once she signed the legal documents to unite the properties under the title of '*Salerno*', she'd have outlived her usefulness to him.

She shrank back into the chair. A feeling of loneliness washed over her. A loneliness so poignant, it threatened to swamp her.

Damn it all, she wouldn't let it. Where was the pleasure in having him around when she hardly saw him, hardly spoke to him? Since the marriage, their former closeness had disintegrated and seemed as distant as the miles between Melbourne and River Bend. At least in the past when he treated her as his little sister, she'd felt warmed by his genuine affection.

On a long sigh, she forced herself from the house and across to Red Earth, carrying a basket with a lunch and vacuum flask of boiling water, packed by Rosa. It had taken her three months to find the courage or inclination to clear out her old home, though she'd promised the house weeks ago to the property managers, Joe and Mary and their family.

Today she prepared to tackle Anna's room, and with shaky fingers slid open the doors of the walk-in wardrobe. Did she imagine it, or did the fragrance of her sister's heady perfume still linger there?

She ran her hand through the rows of lovely gowns with designer labels; the filmy, lacy underwear. Once she had criticized Anna for her extravagances when their Pa struggled financially, but now she felt glad that in her short lifetime, her sister had surrounded herself with, and enjoyed, the things she loved so much.

What would her sister want her to do with the clothing? She decided to consult Rafe, and began packing it into boxes between tissue paper for storage. Perhaps a charity auction for the intensive care unit at the hospital?

As she carefully folded each garment, her attention kept returning to one after-five dress. Red silk, it was fashioned off the shoulder, with a fitted bodice, long, see-through sleeves, and a skirt which molded into the body and flared slightly at the ankle. She held it against her, turning as a model would in front of the cheval mirror. Though it wasn't a gown she'd choose for herself — too flamboyant — she could understand why Anna did. It would make you feel sexy, desirable; a dress which would capture a man's attention. She decided no one else should ever wear it. It belonged utterly to her vivacious sister.

Setting it aside as she held back tears, she began emptying the drawers, admiring several things as she drew them out. Something in a bottom drawer refused to move. She pulled the drawer further out and found several letters wedged into a corner. They were tied with a scarlet ribbon.

Drawing in her breath, she lifted them from their hiding place. Were they love letters from Rafe? With a twist of pain, she resisted the temptation, though her fingers burned to open one. Instead, she tossed them on the bed, trying to ignore them.

But fascinated, her glance kept returning to them. Finally, she picked one up and took a closer look. She gasped. The envelope was not in Rafe's familiar handwriting. Who then? She slipped the letter out and read the opening lines, 'My beautiful Anna'. Her heart racing, she thrust it back into its envelope and tucked the bundle into the upper pocket of her denim overalls with hot and shaky fingers.

Rafe and Pa Dom must never know of their existence. She'd destroy them, burn them.

But she could not destroy her thoughts. Anna had an affair with another man. Was that why she'd kept postponing her marriage to Rafe? She hardly dared think about it, yet knew in her heart it could be. For Anna's beauty, her effervescent nature, drew the men of River Bend to her like parrots to a field of grain.

So what? Her sister would never have offered them more than crumbs. She enjoyed a good time, but Rafe was her man.

Giorgi's heart missed a beat. What nobody knew was that he was *her* man, too.

The Rintoli sisters were so different. Everyone remarked on it. She had her mother's blue eyes, her independent disposition. But when it came to men, it was Anna who inherited her mother's tendency to be carefree and sometimes irresponsible around them. Giorgi arrested her thoughts there. If Rafe saw the letters, as old as they probably were, he could be shattered. She'd burn them at the first opportunity.

By late afternoon she had everything packed for removal. Once the house was cleaned, Joe and his family could move in. She wiped her brow. Mid-spring and the sun had some bite in it. She pulled the blinds and curtains in every room, and in the kitchen poured the last of the boiling water from the flask into a mug. Jiggling a tea bag in it, she glanced around her, probably for the last time. So why didn't she feel anything more than a vague regret for this once bustling room, this once happy home?

She worried about it on the walk home until she found an acceptable answer. The house today was an empty shell, which had harvested the loss of her mother and later her father and sister. Besides, she wasn't leaving her memories of Red Earth and the happy growing-up years behind. She took them with her, forever locked in her heart, there to be called to mind when she chose.

Entering Sunny Valley via the kitchen, Giorgi placed the picnic basket on the bench, then spent an hour with Papa Dom playing cards. Later, she took a shower and changed for dinner. She was pulling a cool blue cotton dress over her head when she heard Rafe's voice ask in hushed tones, 'Is it okay to come in?'

The overalls and underwear she'd discarded still littered the floor. With a few quick tugs her dress fell into place. She smoothed it over her hips. 'Yes.'

As she glanced around, she found him already standing inside. 'You could have knocked,' she said crossly.

'And alert everyone to the fact that I have to knock before I go into my bedroom?'

'Don't you ever tire of this fiasco?' She sighed. She didn't want another discussion today on the matter, so she picked up an earring and began inserting it into her lobe.

'Frequently.' Dull eyes gazed back at her, then lowered to the floor. She followed his glance. Her heart raced.

Dear heaven, a corner of Anna's letters had slipped from the pocket of her discarded overalls. How could she have forgotten about them? Had he noticed? Besieged by questions, she decided she had to somehow retrieve the situation.

Dropping the earring to the floor, she muttered, 'Blast,' and stooped to pick it up, hoping that unnoticed she could edge the letters back into the overalls' pocket. At the same time, he also bent to pick up the earring. Her hand covered the protruding letters. His flashed to lay over it. Hot, her gaze flew to his face to witness fiery eyes.

He lifted her hand, dragging out the package. 'I thought you were hiding something. Love letters from someone? Your chef, perhaps?' The dark hair on his forehead glistened with sweat.

As she stood up, she tried to decide whether or not to agree the letters were to her. It would save him knowing about Anna. About to say yes, she looked down to find him reading the top envelope.

'I can see they're not yours.'

'So do I get an apology?' Anything, she thought, say anything to distract him.

'Where did you get them? Why are you carrying them around?' He waved the letters.

He'd seen they were addressed to Anna. Drawing in her breath, she murmured, 'I'm sorry, I didn't want you to see them.'

'If you didn't want me to see them, why did you toss them on the floor?' He hastened to close the door. 'Rosa could have found them.'

'You're exaggerating, Rafe. They weren't tossed on the floor. They were sticking out of the pocket of my denims. That must have happened while I was getting out of them. Two minutes more and they'd have been safe from prying eyes, but you burst in . . . ' She matched his glance, but the storm in his eyes began to clear.

'Now who's exaggerating? I didn't burst in. But hell, that's not important.

Have you read the letters?'

'Of course not. They were addressed to Anna.'

He flung out his arms. 'But you've guessed they were love letters?'

Giorgi moved quickly to one side to avoid contact with him. 'You knew about them?'

'Not those particular ones.'

Confused, Giorgi began shaking her head, protesting. 'You mean there were others?'

'You may as well know. Yes, I found some when I went across to Red Earth months ago. You remember you asked me once if I'd been through Anna's things and I told you I couldn't because I felt like an intruder.'

She held her breath, nodding.

'That's when I found some letters.'

'They're probably from her school days. Women tend to keep those kinds of things. I know for a fact she had a crush on Tony Conte once. But she loved you. She wouldn't have done anything to . . . '

He flung the letters on the bed and flopped down, raking hair back from his forehead. 'I know she loved me. But imagine how hard it must have been for someone with her vitality and energy to have her destiny mapped out for her from birth. She needed excitement in her life, she was born to party, being with her was never dull. That's what made her so . . . so desirable.'

'You had your future mapped out, too.'

'Yeah, but I've always had a hands-on role with the vineyard. I've had plenty to keep body and mind occupied. Anna lived for a good time.'

'And her little . . . er . . . flings didn't upset you?'

'Sure, at the time they damn near sent me over the edge, but she was honest about them. She'd tell me afterwards she'd been crazy and ask my forgiveness.'

Giorgi sat beside him on the bed, touching him gently on the arm. 'And you always gave it? It must have been torturous for you. I had no idea.'

'The dream, Giorgi, the dream. It mattered to me and it mattered to her.'

'And you didn't doubt you were the only man she truly loved? I know I never did.'

Rafe turned away from her, as if avoiding her searching look. 'No doubts at all. Not one.'

Was he trying to convince himself, or did he have that supreme confidence? As if to answer her thoughts, he added, 'Mind you, there were days when I questioned my weakness, asked myself if I wasn't obsessed with her. But damn it, we're talking here about a few brief little affairs. We all have them.'

'You, too?'

'I've got Italian blood in my veins.'

His laughed sounded phony. Of course, he *was* obsessed with Anna. Giorgi's heart felt as if it were packed in dry ice. How on earth had she been so blind as to chase rainbows, and believe, even vaguely, that one day he might fall in love with her? Though Anna was dead, he was still obsessed with her.

'If only I'd known.' Giorgi raised her brows, her voice sounding strained.

'It wouldn't have made any difference.'

'I could have been there for you, helped you through the rough patches, the lonely times. You were always there for me when I needed someone. It must have been tough, but you hung in there, Rafe.'

'We both did. Your sister deserves some credit, too. She would never have walked away from the dream. Giorgi, you mustn't start judging her. Don't ever let anything muddy her memory. She was a beautiful, vibrant person.'

Giorgi stood up, strolling across to the window and lifting the corner of the lace curtain to peer out. It gave her something to do. 'Do you think the marriage would have worked?' she asked quietly.

'Sure it would have. Once Anna got the itch out of her system, she'd have settled down. We'd have settled down.'

'You didn't have any doubts about her?'

'Not as far as the marriage went. She was always honest with me. She never lied.'

Giorgi tried to convince herself she agreed with Rafe, but it didn't matter now anyway. Still peering out the window, she asked, 'So what happens to the letters?'

Outside someone was mowing the lawn, she heard the whirr whirr of the motor, but the sound failed to drown out her awareness that he was coming to join her by the window. Soon she heard his shallow breathing, imagined his rapid heartbeat, felt the warmth of his arm as it lightly brushed hers. But she continued to stare out, seeing nothing, afraid her emotions might run free and prompt her to reach out and touch him.

'I can't see the point of throwing doubt and confusion over River Bend's big romance now that Anna's dead. We should burn the letters and any others

264

which might turn up.'

'There aren't any more. I've cleaned and packed away everything. You can breathe easily. Nobody will ever know. I intended to burn them anyway so you wouldn't see them.' She gave a shaky laugh. 'But I was so tired and grubby after a day working at Red Earth that I went straight to the shower and forgot about them. Why don't we burn them now?'

She dropped the curtain from her fingers, swinging away from him and strolling towards the fireplace. There she turned back, taking a box of matches from the marble shelf.

'Where are the letters?'

He retrieved them from the bed and walked slowly towards her. 'You don't have to do this,' he said. 'In case you're wondering, I think I know who they're from. I recognize the writing. I partly read the first one I found. You probably think that's pretty low of me, but the ones I discovered earlier weren't tied in ribbon as these are. Just a couple of loose letters. Given Anna's penchant for shopping . . . ' His eyes, when they met hers, asked for forgiveness.

'You thought they were bills. You did the sensible thing and opened them.' She put out her hand and he dropped the letters into it.

'They're from one of the pickers who come every year for the harvest. He's your typical laid-back Aussie. Hard worker, big spender at the bar, good company. I always like him.'

'Will you take him on again next year?' She tossed the letters into the grate.

'I don't see why not. I didn't blame him. Anna bewitched everyone.' A shaft of sunlight caught a single tear glistening on his tanned cheek.

How could he be so forgiving, so God-awful generous? How could his love survive the torment of Anna's affairs? A man of strength, of determination, but where Anna was concerned, a man touched by tragedy.

Giorgi's impulse was to cradle him to

her, to shelter him from his memories. As he bent to the empty grate, she forced herself to stand tall and straight, set against dissolving into the marshmallow mess he sometimes made of her feelings.

With strong, work-hardy hands, he untied the scarlet ribbon and spread out the pages. His thighs strained as he supported himself on his haunches.

'Matches?' He reached out his hand and she placed the box in it.

Burn Anna. You don't deserve such love, such loyalty, such understanding, she almost cried out. *I'd have settled for half as much love as he gave you.*

'Why did she have to die so young?' He seemed to be talking to himself as he struck a match and placed it to the paper. His desolate words brought a halt to her ugly feelings, and compassion reclaimed her heart. She was alive, her sister dead, the scenario tragically shattered. Nobody deserved to die so young. Her selfish denunciation of her sister brought burning tears to the back of her eyes. *I'm sorry, Anna. It's not your fault I fell for your man. In life you were always yourself. Not like me. Pretending. What I have to do now is go back to Melbourne as soon as Dom's all right, and put an end to this charade.*

The flames licked at the paper. It curled under the heat. Picking up the fireside poker, Rafe rearranged the charred remains until only ashes remained. 'Thank goodness that's over,' he said, wiping his brow, rising to his feet.

Over, she thought. How apt. Any chance of a life with Rafe was definitely over. She'd given it her all, and it wasn't enough. She had to move on. How strange, that she suddenly felt a little easier in her mind, now that she'd made the decision.

He turned to her. 'I think I'll have a shower before dinner if you don't need the bathroom for a while.'

She smiled briefly. 'It's all yours.' She strolled across to the dressing table, picked up the gilt-edged brush and began stroking it through her hair, waiting for him to leave. She felt his eyes on her.

'Have I ever told you I love your hair? It lights up the room with its radiance. It lights up your face.'

She ran her tongue along dry lips. It had been a long time since he last paid her a compliment. Was it as long ago as back at her home in Melbourne, she wondered? 'I didn't know you were such a poet, Rafe.'

In the mirror. she saw him approach her. Her body tensed as he came closer. Was he planning to take the brush from her and stroke it through her hair?

He placed his hands on her shoulders, met her glance in the mirror. 'And you're a damned good sport. I don't know what I'd have done without you these last months,' he said.

Her shoulders stiffened under his hold. A good sport? She twisted around on the seat, looking up at him, but her words of derision died on her lips. It

269

wasn't an intended slap in the face; he didn't know how she felt about him. She'd never even hinted that she felt more than sisterly love for him.

And now that she'd made her decision to leave, he must never discover the depth of her feelings.

'Any time,' she managed to say as she stood, walking towards the door. 'I'm going to give Rosa a hand with dinner. See you later.'

'Giorgi . . . '

She turned at the sound of his voice.

'Don't forget what I said about taking time out and going back to Melbourne for a trip. You've earned a break.' He grinned, as if the burning of the letters had seared away the pain, as if the darkness of the past hour had been zapped by the flames.

'I was thinking of taking off after we sign the contract tomorrow.' She blushed briefly at the white lie. She hadn't formulated any time schedule, but remembering her decision, remembering her restaurant opened on Friday evenings, and tomorrow was Friday, she had an urgent need to be down there; an urgent need to throw off the fetters of River Bend.

'Good idea. Will you fly or drive?' He had his hand on the bathroom door.

If he'd asked her to stay, begged her to stay, she'd have found the strength to resist, yet his indifference bruised her heart. 'Fly probably. I'll hire a car down there if I need one,' she said curtly.

'We'll tell Pa tonight at dinner.' He rattled the door handle, impatient, she thought, to get away.

'You do it,' she said, quietly deter-mined to give him the responsibility of explaining, and left.

11

Rafe waited, on edge, for the right moment to tell his father Giorgi was going away. It came after an uncomfortably silent meal, sitting around one end of the long family table sharing a bottle of red wine.

'By the way, Pa, Giorgi will be missing for a day or two. She's got business matters to clear up in Melbourne.' He turned to her. 'You're leaving after our appointment with the solicitors tomorrow, aren't you?'

She nodded.

'I been thinking you need the honeymoon to make the *bambinos*. I no worries now with Rosa. You go too, son.' The crazed lines on Pa Dom's old face deepened as he grinned.

Rafe's attention winged to Giorgi. She shuffled in her chair, her cheeks turning pink.

'Nah.' Rafe held up his arms. 'Melbourne's too cold for a honeymoon this time of year, Pa. As soon as your doctor gives the word, we're off to the north somewhere.'

Rafe poured his father a second glass of red wine.

Rosa rushed across, placing her hand over Dom's glass. 'He already have one drink, Mr. Rafe.'

'Sit down with us, Rosa, and have a drink yourself. This is a celebration. Tomorrow the two properties become one, under the name of Dom's and Bruno's old home in Italy . . . Salerno. And Giorgi's taking a short holiday in Melbourne. A little extra alcohol doesn't hurt now and then,' Rafe said. He was starting to think it might be a damned good idea to get drunk. It had been a helluva day.

Rosa threw up her hands and laughed. 'Oh, Mr. Rafe, how can that be to celebrate if Mrs. Giorgi she go away?'

'Sit down, and don't ask silly

questions. You know that's not what I meant,' he insisted as he poured a glass of wine for her and topped up his own.

'Rosa has a point, Rafe,' Giorgi said. In contrast to Rosa's, Giorgi's laugh sounded forced.

'Women! Always reading things into what men say. You know we'll miss you, Giorgi.' He held his glass in the air. 'So let's drink a toast to the union of Red Earth and Sunny Valley. To our Salerno.' Their glasses clinked.

'Salerno,' Dom said in a harsh whisper. Tears shone in his eyes. 'And to those who gone, who not be here to see it.'

Rafe glanced across at Giorgi. Her bottom lip quivered. Bloody hell, this could turn into a wake, he thought. 'But think how happy Bruno will be up there when the news reaches him. They'll be celebrating at St. Peter's gate. His lifetime dream come true. We made it happen, Pa. Giorgi, you and me. We made it happen. Salerno is safe.' Quickly he replenished his glass, raising it again. 'To the million dollar dream come true.'

Dom fisted his eyes. 'To the dream,' he said gruffly.

As they clinked glasses again, Rafe watched his wife. Her blue eyes had dulled. How unhappy he'd made her. Their relationship had changed so much. Long ago, whenever they spoke, her eyes would shine. She'd reach up, kiss him on the cheek and link her arm into his.

'What've you been up to, little dude?' he'd ask.

She'd strike him gently on the chest. 'You first. What have you and my big sister been up to?' She'd raise her eyebrows and laugh gently, hinting.

Sometimes they sat for ages on the verandah as the night closed about them; or in the orange grove on the tractor, their faces shaded from the sun. And they'd talk about her progress at the university, her plans for the future. He'd joke about her stealing the hearts of the other students, her roles in the campus plays. She was the complete little sister. He groaned. What had he done to her by forcing the marriage? What had he done to their relationship? She'd lost her independence, her spirit; they'd lost that special bond.

She'd tried to hide her unhappiness. And to his discredit, he'd tried to ignore it. Long before this he'd noticed the change in her; her lack of surety, her failure to make decisions, the artificial smile. Only the progress in the legal arrangements for the properties sparked her moods.

But to keep the dream alive he'd pushed aside his doubts and pursued it, persuading himself she'd be all right in the end; she had the resources, the toughness.

He downed another drink in two quaffs, rose and retrieved a second bottle of wine from the dresser. 'Let's make a night of it, Pa,' he growled.

'You do whatever you like, Rafe,' Giorgi said, rising with haste, her tone adamant, uncompromising. 'But Pa's had enough. He's going to bed. Rosa, would you mind?'

The old man patted her arm as he left the room on his stick. 'You always sensible one, Giorgi. I sleep tonight now we got Salerno. You, too, little one?'

After he left the room with Rosa, Giorgi closed the door, turning back to Rafe with fire in her eyes. 'Get drunk if that's your way of handling things, but don't come staggering into the room in the middle of the night falling over everything. Sleep somewhere else.'

Though he had drank only a few glasses, the wine, or was it his conscience, made him react angrily. 'I always sleep somewhere else. I could find my way into that bloody dressing room blindfolded.'

'Don't come through *my* bedroom. Find your way into another room from now on,' she cried. 'The property deal's been clinched, the dream a reality as you just said. You don't need me any longer. All that talk about a honeymoon up north made me crawl. I felt ashamed. I hate this damned pretence, the lies.' Her hands swept to her head. 'They have to end, Rafe.'

As she slammed the door, he pushed the unopened bottle of wine aside. Of course he needed her around. He'd always needed her. In her absences, he'd looked forward to her coming home. Always known she would be there, at arm's length. Why hadn't he realized that before? He got up, eager to explain to her how important she was to him. But he stopped at the unopened bedroom door. If he went to her now she'd think it was a ploy to win back her cooperation; to keep her at Salerno until Dom got his medical clearance.

He stood there, damning himself for his insensitivity, for doing all the taking. What had he given up in this arrangement? A big fat zero.

More than anything he wanted to put the sunshine back into her eyes when she looked at him. But how? There was only one way. He'd give her back her freedom.

Somehow he'd make Pa understand the marriage hadn't worked. That after Anna died, only one part of the dream was ever going to be possible.

He'd tell her tomorrow when he dropped her off at the airport after the signing.

He kicked off his boots and crashed on to the bed in the guest room. He didn't give a damn who found out he didn't sleep with his wife.

★ ★ ★

It was almost ten o'clock on Friday evening when Giorgi pushed open the door of Giorgina's restaurant and breathed in the rich, tangy smells of food. As she stepped inside, a sense of freedom overtook her and she almost danced across the crowded room to the music.

So many clients, so much chatter and laughter. She was back where she belonged.

Jessica, one of the waiters, caught her

attention, greeting her with a beaming smile and a wave of her hand.

Making her way to the kitchen, Giorgi slipped quietly into the area and stood there, observing, happy, waiting for someone to look up and notice her. From behind, Nathan spoke.

'Giorgi. Is it really you?'

Startled, she swung around. His wide grin warmed her as she held back the urge to run to his side. Better not to let anyone sense her happiness at being here, her disaster of a marriage. 'Nathan. It's so good to see you.'

The palms of their hands slapped together, once, twice. 'Why didn't you let me know you were coming?'

'I decided to surprise you.' She flicked a strand of hair from her face.

He raised his brows. 'To check up on us I suppose?' His face creased with amusement.

'What else? I'll help out. Is there a spare apron anywhere around here?' She glanced about her, laying her purse on a bench.

'Not tonight. We've got everything in hand. Tonight you dine in your own restaurant in style. I'll take you to a table, and join you there for a late supper.'

He placed her purse back in her hand, put his arm under her elbow and led her back into the restaurant.

'I can't believe I'm letting you do this,' she said, smiling.

'You're not letting me, boss. You haven't got a choice. You look tired.'

'Thanks very much.'

'Well you do. What the hell have they been doing to you up there?'

So the strain of the last few months showed. 'It's called Giorgina's deprivation. I missed you all so much,' she said, forcing a lilt to her voice.

'So sit down and stop making a fuss. I'll bring you a glass of white wine, and a menu.'

'I'm not hungry.'

'You're eating something. One of my pastas.'

As she slid into a small alcove table

for two, she touched his arm. 'Is my weariness that obvious?'

'You look thinner and paler than when you left. To be honest, I expected to see you radiant with health, and sporting a Sunset Country suntan.' He sat down beside her. 'Say, you're not . . . um . . . er . . . having a . . . pregnant are you? Sorry, that's a bit personal isn't it? You don't have to answer.'

She curved her lips. 'No, I'm not. I've had a lot on my mind these past months with the wedding and Papa Dom's health, and getting Red Earth cleared out. Did you mention a white wine?'

'One white wine coming up. I'll join you in . . . ' He glanced at his watch, tapping its face. 'Fifteen minutes.' He edged out of the seat.

Barney, the drink waiter, arrived only minutes later with a bottle of wine and a Luna Park smile, followed by Jessica who also greeted her with a similar grin and handed her the menu.

'I see tagliatelle is on tonight. Just a

282

small serving please, Jessica, with Nathan's wonderful tomato and mushroom sauce.'

As she lounged back in her seat, sipping her wine, Giorgi thought how right all this felt. *Thank goodness I found out before it was too late.* But what did she mean by too late? *Before you made a fool of yourself and offered yourself to Rafe.* The answer winged back to her. *Forget Rafe, forget Salerno and Pa Dom. Forget mark two of the dream. Give yourself a break.*

Nathan joined her shortly afterwards and they talked endlessly about the restaurant and its people. Once she had thought they might get together. They had the food industry in common, enjoyed going to the gym, visiting new markets. He'd made advances, but somehow it didn't happen for her.

She didn't quite know what she expected from the relationship, but she did know she wasn't falling in love with him. He didn't have dark, gentle eyes which sometimes turned fiery, but as suddenly softened and relaxed. He didn't have a bounty of black hair which flopped across his broad forehead, or a body which spoke of strength.

Before it went too far she'd told Nat they could only ever be good friends. He appreciated her candor he said at the time, but seemed flat for a day or two afterwards. She'd hurt him, but he'd bounced back. He was the type of guy who was never fazed for too long. A refreshing change from the emotional roller-coaster she traveled with the men in her family. Not that they weren't endearing and explicitly open, but it could become tiresome.

'You know,' he said now, as if he'd been tuned in to her thoughts. 'I didn't give up hoping one day you'd change your mind about us. Your husband's a lucky son-of-a-gun. I hope he realizes it.'

She smiled gently, but said nothing. In a few months time he would find out her husband didn't realize what a lucky so-and-so he was. But tonight she continued to give credence to the charade.

With the last client gone, the tables cleared and the candles snuffed out, several of the staff gathered around her, drinking to her good health, making her feel wanted in a special way, until weariness finally claimed her.

'Must go, but I'll be in tomorrow. And no protests, Nat. I promise I won't get in your way or try to change your menus or your plans. But I insist on being here.'

'We can find you plenty to do. How long are you down for?' he asked.

'I'm due to go back on Monday.' Not *home*, she thought with a heavy heart. Living at Happy Valley had never felt like being home.

The weekend was crowded with activities. The sun shone. She lunched with her university friends at South-bank, overlooking the river.

'Didn't we tell you black underwear was the go?' Michelle laughed. They all laughed. 'What's he like in bed? Romantic?'

Giorgi stroked her heated cheeks, forcing her lips to curve and let the lie through. 'Sensational. We Italians invented the word romance.'

They hooted. 'How often do you do it?'

'None of your business.'

'What a legend your man must be. You're blushing.'

'It's a reflection of the sun. Isn't it time we talked about someone else's love life?'

In the afternoon she went through the restaurant books with her accountant, and on Saturday and Sunday nights, Nathan insisted she act as hostess.

Her break came to an end much too soon. On Monday morning she arranged to meet Nat at the restaurant to discuss a few business matters.

'When are you coming back again? Get that husband of yours to take time off soon so you can spend a week or two down here next time,' he said, holding her hands, kissing her cheek as she prepared to leave. 'You smell nice,' he added.

If only his eyes upon her could unsettle her heart even vaguely. But they didn't, though she enjoyed the compliment. 'Doesn't every woman you kiss?'

'Not this good. We miss you.'

'As I said earlier, I'll be back every couple of weeks from now on. But I'll keep in touch and let you know next time when I'm coming.'

The break had convinced her to slowly increase her absences from the Bend, so that when she left for good, it wouldn't cause astonishment or too much wailing and gnashing of teeth.

'Take care, Giorgi. At least you're going home with a bit more color in your cheeks. Have you enjoyed it?'

'Like crazy.' She hadn't meant to say anything to raise his eyebrows and put questions into his minds. The truth had slipped out.

'I suspected as much. You're finding it hard-going up there, aren't you? I haven't got any right to say this, but if Rafe isn't treating you right . . .'

'You're wrong, Nat. Everything's fine on that score,' she broke in. She'd become quite adept at lying when she had to. 'I think it's the after-affects of losing Pa and my sister, and the scare Pa Dom gave us. It's finally caught up with me. But I feel better after this R and R.'

'Hardly that. We worked you pretty hard.' He tucked her arm into his, walking her to the door of the restaurant. 'I'm still interested in buying this place. So if you ever think of selling it, you'll give me first refusal, won't you?'

'Of course.' She climbed into the waiting taxi, turning to wave goodbye to Nat as it pulled out from the curve and was soon at the airport passenger terminal.

★   ★   ★

At the Bend, it was late afternoon. Rosa, Pa Dom and Rafe sat on the shady side of the verandah waiting for her. As her taxi moved through the property entrance, she saw the new signage hanging from a cross bar above the gate — 'Salerno', it said in dark, bold letters. It had gone up so quickly, Giorgi guessed it had been painted and stored away for a long time, perhaps even before her Pa had died. She tried to tell herself how pleased he would have been, but felt only the emptiness his sudden departure had left in her heart.

As she traversed the long drive to the house, she sighed, her stomach knotting. Here she was, back to the old routine, as if the last couple of days hadn't happened. There would be pressing kisses, arms waving, good cheer, the pretense that everything was as it should be.

Rafe ignored the verandah steps and hurtled from it in one long stride. He was beside the vehicle, opening the door, helping her out, his tanned, bare arm warm against her skin. She'd thought as little about him as possible while away, but back home, he effortlessly reapplied the restraints on her heart with his broad, dark-eyed grin; his heady male scent.

Her sense of freedom fell away in an instant.

He touched his lips to hers, her heart racing, her hand refusing to take orders from her mind. She stroked his beloved face and returned his kiss. Dear heaven, she could hardly believe her joy at seeing him.

'Happy to be home?' he whispered, his breath feathering through her hair, dislodging it into wisps which curled back onto one cheek. 'You look wonderful. You've got that beautiful blowtorch-blue light back in your eyes.' His dark eyes searched hers, alive, she suspected, with hope. 'Could it be that you missed us?'

Dragged back to the position from which she had so briefly escaped, of loving him and wanting him, but knowing the impossibility of it, her mind rebelled. If she were to bring off her return to the city, she couldn't give him any reason to hope. Still she didn't want to sound bitter or unkind, because clearly he was happy to have her back.

'I had a wonderful time, Rafe. I'm planning to go down regularly from now on. The business is thriving and Nathan needs backup on special occasions.'

Concern darkened the pupils of his eyes. 'I understand.' He picked up her overnight bag, slinging it carelessly over one shoulder and waving his arm towards the verandah. 'Your fans await you, *signora*,' he said with a show of levity his taut features didn't share.

She looked up as Joe and Mary, carrying a tray full of food, followed by Mario and his wife, arrived on the verandah from inside the house. Giorgi's next sentence stuck in her throat. The last thing she wanted was a welcoming committee. At the same time she felt both a traitor, and trapped. But somehow she managed to manufacture a smile and greet everyone.

After what seemed an era, the visitors left, and Pa Dom retired. Giorgi returned to the verandah to wait for Rafe, who had left on his regular nightly inspection of the property. As he approached, torch in hand, a light wind soughed through the eucalypts growing close to the house and a limb rattled against the spouting, startling her. She felt sick with anticipation, restless with the need to tell Rafe tonight that she could no longer go on pretending.

'Still up,' he said casually, hardly glancing in her direction, as he flopped on to the verandah's edge and began tugging off his elastic-sided boots. 'I thought you'd be tired after your long day.'

'Not too tired to talk.'

He turned his head quickly in her direction. 'Then I'm not too tired to listen.'

'It's Pa Dom's eightieth birthday in four week's time.'

He nodded. 'Yes. Rosa's planning a party.'

'I thought she might. I'll stay on until then. Afterwards we should make plans to tell him I'm going back to live in Melbourne. It's my home. It's where I belong. I'm sure of that now.'

'Permanently you mean?'

'Yes.' Her voice softened to a whisper. 'This is hard for me. You'll never know how hard it is, but I have to do it. I can't live like this. I'm not a quitter, but this isn't natural. I hate the deceit.'

Rafe came to her side. The subtle fragrance of her perfume threatened to snare his plans. He'd intended to comfort her, hold her hand, but aroused by her loveliness in the evening light, he changed his mind and took the chair opposite her.

'I know. I've seen what it's done to you. For a minute back there when you got out of the taxi, you looked so happy.

I thought maybe, just maybe, you were glad to be back. But you soon put me right on that.'

'I'm desperately sorry, but if I'd had some part in running the properties. Instead, I've become an onlooker . . . ' She gestured with her hands. 'I'm used to running a business, making decisions by myself. I'm not like Anna. Anna always needed people around her. I don't, I need challenges.'

He gestured with leaden arms, for he had no answers. He attempted a joke. 'I would have thought living with me has been a challenge.'

'I haven't been living *with* you. I've been an appendage, living *alongside* you and your father.'

There was nothing he could say to alter the truth. 'You don't have to spell it out. The family has always asked too much of you. But it's big brother Rafe you're talking to now, little dude, so don't fret yourself. I understand where you're coming from. I've always understood you. I've always known I shouldn't have made that trip to Melbourne. I had no right.'

Giorgi dashed hair back from her face, pushing deeper into her chair. *You might think you understand me, but you've always had one very big blind spot where I'm concerned. And thank heaven you have. I couldn't bear seeing the look of pity in your eyes if you knew how I really feel about you.*

He went on. 'After you left I made up my mind to give you an easy out if you wanted it. I promised you that back in Melbourne, didn't I? I'm grateful for the time you've taken out of your life to see the merger come to fruition. It's one positive to salvage out of this damned awful mess, isn't it?' He edged forward in his chair.

She began to choke up, to wish he wasn't being so accepting, so thoughtful. If he'd ranted at her, she could have sparked up the energy to defend her decision. 'Of course I do. I . . . ' she managed before her voice cracked.

'Can you survive the next four

weeks? Say if you can't.'

The compassion in his voice brought a rush of tears to sting the back of her eyes. She choked them back and stood on wobbly legs, anxious to escape before she began to cry openly. 'You know me,' she joked, 'I'll survive. I'm that tough little dude you used to like so much.'

The words sounded unconvincing, almost mocking. She tried to bolster her strength with the thought that she'd had a lifetime of playing tough where her feelings for him were concerned. 'We'll work out what we're going to do, how we're going to tell Pa Dom.' She looked down at her fingernails. 'I think we should do it together,' she found the will to add.

'You don't have to. I can do it.'

'No. We're in this together.' She faked a yawn, desperate to close off the conversation and escape. 'I'm off to bed. It's been a long day. Goodnight, and thanks for making it so easy for me.'

As she opened the flywire door to enter the house, he said. 'We should start preparing Pa straight away, otherwise the news will be too much of a shock.'

She turned back to him. 'He's not a fool. He'll guess something's going on when I'm away so often. I did make it clear to you didn't I? I plan to spend lots of time in Melbourne from now on.'

'Crystal clear. Would you mind turning out the verandah light on your way in?' he said. 'I'm going to stay out here for a while. It's a lovely evening.'

She pressed the switch, the electric light fading. She spoke into the gloom. 'I'm relieved we've made a decision. I've always hated uncertainty.'

As Rafe's eyes became accustomed to the light of the late evening, he fisted back tears. Momentarily, after she arrived back, it seemed as if she couldn't wait to be in his arms. And God help him, when her hand brushed so tenderly over his face, he wanted to take her there and then, with the world looking on. If she hadn't followed up with those cold words that she planned to visit Melbourne regularly, who knows . . .

12

He had to face it. The strain of not touching his wife was playing funny buggers with his life, blurring his vision of day-to-day activities. At times he found it difficult to concentrate when working in the vineyards. Vivid images floated into his head. Not of Anna, but of Giorgi, of her body, of her creamy skin, of the breasts he sometimes glimpsed when she wore one of those skimpy little tops. They really turned him on, making it necessary for him to shove his hands into the pockets of his trousers to hide his feelings.

One afternoon, when she strolled into the kitchen, her nipples outlined against the blue cotton top, her tanned, shapely legs bare to the top of brief shorts, he'd had an alarmingly quick response. And damn it, all he was wearing were shorts without pockets.

He'd turned back to the sink, taking a long glass of water while he tried to concentrate on something going on outside the window.

At most inopportune times, he found himself burning to fondle her breasts, claim her nipples. Claim her body. He'd almost turned over the tractor while clearing the other day, missing the deep ruts because he'd been thinking of her. And at night he lay in his bed willing himself not to give into his urge to go to her. He rarely thought of Anna these days, and when he did it seemed that what he had had with her was something ethereal, other-worldly, without substance. Always a tantalizing touch away, and wasn't that what Giorgi had become?

He slapped the palm of his hand to his head, reminding that she planned to leave in four or five weeks. It was right for her. It was bloody right for him, too. He couldn't go on like this. They could have the marriage annulled — he laughed harshly in the privacy of the darkness. It couldn't be called a marriage when it hadn't been consummated. He'd find himself a local girl to marry. One who fitted into the River Bend community: one who'd give him babies. What good had the merger of the properties been if there were no children to inherit Salerno? Giorgi obviously didn't care who owned it. Her career was what mattered to her.

First he had to get over the big hurdle — his Pa. The old boy's health had improved markedly, and given that the properties were secure, would probably continue to do well. He'd begun to walk out to the vineyards in the mornings and spend time working with Rafe. They'd even managed to forestall his complaints about the lack of progress on the *bambino* front, by getting in with statements at breakfast such as, 'Sorry Pa, no news today.'

Suppose Dom thought Giorgi was infertile? He probably wouldn't complain then about their separation. *No you don't. Don't even think about it.*

There can't be any more lies, no more deceptions. Your Pa has to learn the truth, learn to live with it.

He punched the air, began thinking positively, to plan for the day Giorgi wasn't here. His heart missed a beat at the thought. Move on, he ordered himself. You have to make it easy for her to go.

They'd make a start on establishing the rift between them. He might move out of their bedroom suite into another room. That would send the right message if nothing else did. Standing up, he leapt the verandah steps. He no longer felt tired or worn down by the dilemma as he strode across the lawn towards the vineyards.

The Sunset Country had had good winter rains, followed quickly by warm spring days, and a month ago the sunshine had worked up a summer sting. The vines had broken into leaf. The first crop at Salerno would be a bumper one. That had to be a plus for everyone. Nothing made him feel stronger, happier, than walking amongst the grapes, lifting a bunch of the fruit and examining it. Soon it would be ready to sample and then to harvest.

Soon Giorgi would be gone.

★ ★ ★

As Giorgi dressed for Pa Dom's eightieth birthday party, a wave of guilt overwhelmed her. In a day or two she and Rafe would sit down with the old man and tell him everything. The reason they married, and the reason for the annulment they would seek.

The past four weeks had been trying. Dom constantly watched her and asked questions. The most difficult to answer was, 'You got a sickness, you send Rafe sleep in other room?'

The old man hadn't accepted what they'd hoped appeared obvious.

'No, I'm fine.' Frustrated, she'd tried to give him another hint that things weren't right between them. 'You'll have to ask Rafe that. He has all the answers. Ours has never been a partnership,' she said rather caustically.

'You go to the citta all the time. What you expect? And'a you bring Rafe a sickness from there, eh?'

She'd sighed. 'No. I'm not sick and I've not given Rafe anything, Pa.' Would they ever be able to make him understand? 'I have to go back to check on my business. I've got a lot of money tied up in it. Now, stop growling and ask your son why he's sleeping in another room.'

She'd patted and kissed his old cheek and warned herself to stay calm and not let his persistent questions get to her. Why wasn't Rafe ever around to do any of the hard explaining?

She'd made a mental note to insist he start spelling it out to Pa that the marriage was in freefall. Leaving it to the last minute would be far too great a risk to the old man's condition.

The only thing that had her feeling she'd made progress was her ritual of crossing off each day as it passed in the diary she kept in her bedroom drawer.

The fact was she and Rafe had avoided one another since her return from that first visit to Melbourne. They met only for meals, and the occasional obligatory social function. And then he was coldly courteous.

As they'd planned, he acted the husband increasingly disaffected by his wife's city lifestyle, and he did it very convincingly. Only Pa seemed to miss the point. Giorgi had begun to wonder if he did it deliberately because he refused to believe that a Rintoli and a Guardiani weren't meant for each other.

Her weekly trips to Melbourne kept her sane. Even in the city air, clogged as it was with petrol fumes and humanity, she breathed more easily than in the wide empty spaces of the Sunset Country.

Tonight she would again contrive to bring Serena Silvagni and Rafe together. Earlier she'd decided Serena would make him an ideal partner.

The daughter of the family on the

citrus block closest to Salerno, she worked as a receptionist at a local motel, had dark, lively eyes, long black hair and a happy laugh. What made her eminently suitable for Rafe was the fact that she fitted so well into the close-knit community. He, she had decided, needed uncomplicated, cheerful company, after her lousy attempts at fitting into his life.

She dragged her mind back to deciding what she should wear. As she pushed aside the clothes in her wardrobe, her hand stalled at Anna's glamorous red dress-the one she'd kept on impulse. *Why not wear it*? This would be her last big occasion at the Bend. She took it down, holding it against her. Its color did something for her complexion. The strain of the last months had left her thin and in the face, pale, except for the dark smudges under her eyes.

She stepped into the dress, urging it up over her hips and breasts, slipping her arms into the see-through sleeves, and secured the back zip with a quick upward tug. It was almost a perfect fit, perhaps a little too long, but a pair of high-heeled gold sandals would fix that. And, of course, on Anna it would have revealed more of her breasts.

She applied light make-up, fluffed up her hair with her hand, and stood back from the mirror to assess the result. Daring, she thought, wiggling around in the tight-fitting skirt. Not at all her image, but what the hell!

With a wry smile she decided she would be painted the scarlet woman anyway by the community once they learned she'd left Rafe and returned to the city. Like mama, like *bambino*, they'd say of her. Giorgi could live with that. But it hurt when she let herself think how much harder it would be on Rafe because this was his home. Pitying eyes, behind the hands comments — he'd feel them all and resent it with a passion.

A knock came to the door. 'Who is it?' she asked.

'Rafe. Are you ready? Pa's left with Mary and Joe. He didn't want to be late for his party.'

'Coming.' After a last quick glance in the mirror, she slipped her feet into the gold sandals and picked up her black wallet before hurrying to the door. She hadn't been inside the bedroom alone with Rafe since she told him she was leaving. She preferred it that way. It kept her crazy heart from questioning her decision.

As she opened the door she avoided his eyes — another of her measures to keep her feelings in check — for when he looked at her she couldn't avoid seeing her doubts and uncertainties mirrored there. It always touched her and reactivated a feeling of guilt.

Tonight she avoided his eyes but could not escape his sharp intake of breath; the sound of his anger when he demanded, 'What the hell are you doing in that dress?'

Her gaze flew to his eyes. Flames burned there. Anger, and something else. Was it passion, hatred? Dear heaven what had she done. If it were hate she saw . . .

'It was Anna's. I . . . ' she whispered.

'I damn well know who's it was. So why are you wearing it? You look ridiculous.' He gripped her shoulder, forcing her back into the room with powerful arms. 'Get out of it. Now. There's no way you're wearing it in public.' He released her. Glared down at her, from what seemed a great height. Pointed a finger at her. 'Do you hear me? Take it off, Giorgi. You're not Anna, and you never will be.'

Giorgi stepped away from him; from the fiery stare, the tightly drawn lips, and hit out. 'Surely you can't believe I was trying to be my sister. Why would I? Because she had so many admirers and received all the attention in our families? You know none of that was overly important to me.' *Not even because she had you*, she dared not add. 'I happen to like who I am and my life, even if you don't.' Her voice rose.

He raised his arms. 'Don't put words in my mouth. Who you are and how the family treated you is nothing to do with this. Now, get out of the dress. You're not wearing it to the party.'

'I don't take orders from you or anyone else.' With mocking laughter, she dropped on to the seat of the dressing table and spoke to his image in the mirror.

'Grow up, Giorgi,' he growled.

She edged around to face him. 'Now we're getting down to the root of the trouble, aren't we, Rafe?' she said quietly. 'That's what needles you about me. I did grow up. I don't depend on you for advice, or to get me out of scrapes and things as Anna did. I'm beginning to think you enjoyed her dependence on you. Playing the forgiving hero. You encouraged it, didn't you?'

She watched as his face contorted. He turned his back on her and gripped the bed post, before swinging back to face her. 'I was raised to believe that's what men are for. For women to lean on.'

'Oh come on. This is me you're talking to. You can't pretend you haven't moved into today's world, because you know damn well many women have very successful careers these days. They're entitled to go after a goal. It was you, Rafe Guardiani, you, who encouraged me to go to university and persuaded my father to let me. You, who guided me towards independence and taught me 'ambition' wasn't a dirty word.'

The fire no longer flared in his dark eyes; they were full of pain as they looked dully back at her. 'Not all women are like you. Anna wasn't.'

Her anger melted as his suffering touched her. She stood up and walked across to him, her stomach churning with confusion. Her head told her to keep her distance, but her heart compelled her go to him, to say something, to do something to ease his grief. 'She was a real woman. You still miss her, don't you?'

Close to him, so close she heard his intake of breath. So close, if she reached out she could run the tips of her fingers over his eyelids, drop his dark, curling lashes over them, shut out the pain and kiss them until it disappeared. But he backed away from her.

The agonizing reminder that she didn't have Anna's access to his heart pulled her up with a start. She'd been about to make a fool of herself.

'It will all be over after tomorrow, Rafe. Pa will know everything, and I'll be gone soon after that. We're tense tonight, saying things we don't mean, hurting one another. We mustn't part like this.' She reached out and touched him lightly on the arm. 'It was thoughtless of me to wear the dress. I'll change into something else and we can be on our way.'

As she hurried across to the en suite, he rasped, 'Don't you want to know why I'm upset about that damned dress?'

Surprised at the renewed anger in his voice, she faced him, sighing. 'I thought I did, but if you need to get something off your chest, I'm listening, though frankly I'm beyond caring about anything. All I want to do at the moment is to get through tonight and tomorrow.'

'Anna wore that dress the night we finally fixed on a wedding date.' His voice rose, 'She was especially bubbly, full of life and plans for our future . . . Seeing you in . . . '

'Brought it all back.' Giorgi chipped in, feeling as if she wanted to clap her hands over her ears. She could only take so much of being reminded again and again that she wasn't Anna.

'Forget it. The dress looks awful on me.' She pulled the door behind her, dragging off the offensive garment, stepping out of it and flinging it into the dressing room. What had possessed her to wear it? A show of independence? A 'who cares' attitude? She could see now she'd given into a whim.

Trembling with disappointment and

frustration, she raked through her clothes in the wardrobe and dragged a simple, black dress with a short skirt from its hanger. After slipping it over her head, she reorganized stray strands of hair, retouched her make-up, and taking several deep breaths, reentered the room.

He rose quickly from the bed, standing tall, regal in his dark dinner jacket. His tight lips eased into the suggestion of a smile, lips that were meant for laughter, and kisses, but not for her. Sadness crept into her heart. She froze, her heart standing still, as she warded off the overwhelming need to be in his arms. The 'who cares' attitude she'd fought so hard to win was again in danger of collapsing.

'Look Giorgi, about the dress . . . about what I said. I don't want you to think . . . '

'Can we forget it? Let's not go over old ground again.'

'You can beg off tonight if you want. I'll say you're not feeling well. Heaven knows, I've given you reason enough.'

'And miss Dom's party? I couldn't do that.'

Moving across to the dressing table, she opened her jewelry box and took a gold locket bracelet from it to add to the gold chain necklace and earrings she already wore. With shaky fingers, she struggled to clip it around her left wrist under his steady appraisal.

'We haven't discussed exactly when to tell Pa you're going. We could do it tomorrow morning at breakfast. Is that soon enough?'

'It seems a pity to burst his bubble so soon after his birthday, but there's no point in waiting.' She kept her attention on her bracelet, avoiding his eyes.

'And we tell him all?'

'I've been thinking about that. Perhaps as much as he needs to know. I wouldn't want to hurt him unnecessarily. If we could play down the fact that we did it for him, it might ease any guilty feelings he might have. I suggest we say we hoped it would work for us.'

'It's not untrue. I always hoped that, Giorgi.' He gestured uselessly.

She nodded. 'Me, too, but we were expecting a miracle.' She snapped the bracelet catch into place and retrieved a black jacket from a chair. He came forward, took it and held it for her. His breath whispered across her cheek as she shrugged into it.

'And miracles only happen to other people?'

She held herself taut. 'We've already had our share of miracles. Pa got better. The property's safe for you.'

'Hardly a miracle. It cost you a great deal.'

She faked a smile. 'It cost both of us.'

'So this will be our last night out,' he said, as she hurried towards the bedroom door, desperate to place distance between them. 'Let's make it a happy one.'

Giorgi shook her head. 'We can't. Remember people have to start suspecting this is an unhappy marriage. We have to keep up the act.'

'Between us I mean. We can try to recapture some of the special affection that existed between us once, can't we?' He took her arm, guiding her through the door and along the passageway.

His touch, the scent of him, sent unnerving messages firing through her. She pushed forward, freeing herself, trying to block out her feelings.

'I don't think we can ever get back to where we were, Rafe. But I hope we'll always be friends.'

'That won't change. You've always been my dearest friend, always will be.'

Giorgi thought it had already changed. And once she returned to Melbourne, slowly she would cut off anything but business contact with the family at Salerno. It was too unsettling to be near Rafe, to hear his voice, to see the gentleness reserved for her in his dark eyes, to feel the warmth of his touch when he greeted her. It was too damned hard.

They drove to the Princess Royal Hotel in awkward silence, punctuated only by Rafe's frequent cursing against other drivers on the road. Giorgi had grown used to his verbal, but harmless abuse of every other motorist on the River Bend roads, and settled her mind to how she could bring Serena and Rafe together tonight.

As it happened, everything fell into place without any prompting from her. Serena ran to meet them in the hotel foyer, bubbling with the news her brother, an old school friend of Rafe's, was in town. Seizing Rafe by the arm she trotted him off to meet Aldo, and when next Giorgi sighted them, Serena and Rafe were dancing together.

Giorgi stayed close to Pa Dom for most of the evening. She gave him all her attention, because she wanted him to remember his birthday and her with love on their last night together. She even managed to get him onto the dance floor.

'When you dance with your husband, little Giorgina?' he asked.

'He's having such a good time with

Serena. She's an excellent dancer, and such a nice girl, isn't she Pa?'

His wily blue eyes glinted. 'She not his woman, but she good. She not go to citta all time.'

'And I not a proper Italian girl, eh?' She laughed and ran her hand over his deeply etched cheek. But in her heart she felt joyless. When he learned the truth, the man who'd been a second father to her would be crushed. Somehow, she prayed silently, he would find the will to understand and forgive; the strength to accept the news and keep going.

Someone rang a bell, called for attention. 'Come on, Pa,' Giorgi said, 'It looks as if it's speech time.' As she led him back to the table where a huge birthday cake sat on a silver tray, she heard Rafe's voice above the crowd.

'Can we have a little bit of shush, please?' Her attention focused on the stage, where he stood at a stationary microphone, tall, erect, darkly handsome, his hair falling onto his forehead.

Next her glance found Serena, whose eyes shone as she looked up at him. Why hadn't Giorgi noticed before how the woman felt about Rafe? It might have saved them all a lot of heartache.

Serena wasn't first or second choice as a wife for Pa Dom's son, but in all probability the best choice. The thought eased her foreboding about telling him tomorrow, but at the same time she experienced a stabbing pain of loss. She quelled her irrational, ambivalent feelings, joined the congratulations and singing, and helped the old man to cut the cake.

Shortly after midnight, Giorgi accompanied Dom and Rosa home, claiming weariness after a fictitious viral infection, and the need to get the old man to bed. He had celebrated by imbibing a little too much wine.

She urged Rafe quite openly in a barbed voice to stay on as he was obviously enjoying himself. He took the hint, and with a shrug said, 'I intended to stay. I'm having a great night.'

As she left, the lights dimmed, music with a slow beat began, and he turned to Serena. Giorgi stayed only long enough to see him take her by the hand as they drifted onto the dance floor. *I don't care. I'm not jealous. It's what I want*, she repeated over and over under her breath, as she left with Pa. But when the car entered Salerno and pulled up outside the house, she still hadn't convinced herself.

If only her love didn't go beyond her knowing, beyond her understanding. If only it wasn't so deeply implanted in her heart that it tore at her very being to walk away from him.

She crawled into bed, at first glad of the darkness and the sanctuary, but soon she listened restlessly for Rafe's return. Though she heard his unmistakable footsteps along the passageway in the early hours, and knew he'd arrived home safely, sleep still eluded her. Finally, she got up, tip-toed into the dressing room and quietly reached down a suitcase from the wardrobe. As she began packing clothes into it, she noted the duvet and linen Rafe used on the daybed had been neatly folded and stored at one end of the robe.

How long was it since he'd moved into another room? Long enough to alert even the most unobservant person, long enough to alarm Pa Dom, yet he had hardly questioned her about it. Had she and Rafe been deluding themselves? Did the old man already know the truth? In a way she hoped he did, for it would make tomorrow so much easier.

She planned to leave day after tomorrow. *And tomorrow was already here*, she thought wryly, folding her jeans and laying them in the case. Soon it would all be over. *The deceit, the hypocrisy, the hope that sometimes refused to listen to practical argument.*

★ ★ ★

Giorgi had packed her bags through the sleepless night. She waylaid Rafe on his way to breakfast and informed him she planned to leave today once she was certain Dom had accepted the news.

He'd nodded and walked on.

She straightened her shoulders outside the kitchen, told herself to stay calm, to ease her pulsing heart. The time to break the news to Dom had finally arrived.

How would Rafe handle things? She advanced into the room after taking a deep breath. He looked up at her, running a hand through his hair, dislodging it. The dark signs of weariness beneath his eyes contrasted with the summer sunshine that streamed in through the window. It caught a glass of orange juice that glinted back at Giorgi, temporarily obscuring her vision. She blinked a couple of times, vaguely aware as she did, that Rosa fussed about Pa and Rafe holding a packet of cereal in one hand.

Usually she sat opposite Rafe. Today, before entering, she'd decided to sit beside him to avoid eye contact. If he started to weep, she'd probably join him.

The breakfast was interspersed by periods of what seemed like unnatural jollity about last night's party, and long, awkward silences, broken only by Rosa's comings and goings. Giorgi's stomach knotted as the minutes crept by. What if Pa had another heart attack when they told him?

The waiting grew unbearable. Surely everyone heard her heart pounding like the wildness of an angry sea. She elbowed Rafe, and then stood up, pouring herself a second cup of coffee from the percolator on the stove. From a distance, she caught his attention, tilted her head, once, twice, indicating as clearly as she could with body language, *What are you waiting for? I can't stand this terrible waiting.*

'Rosa, when you leave, would you mind closing the door. We have some business matters to discuss,' Rafe said, an authority in his voice which sent the housekeeper scurrying out.

Dom looked up suddenly as Rosa secured the door behind her with an overstated click. Giorgi returned to her chair, leaving the freshly poured coffee behind.

'Giorgi and I have something to tell you, Pa,' Rafe began.

The old man's wrinkles creased, his lips parted, his blue eyes shone. 'The *bambino*. You get the *bambino*. I knew the dream, it finally come if I hold the faith and pray hard.'

Giorgi closed her eyes, shuddered with despair. Rafe's opening words couldn't have been more ill-considered. He ought to have foreseen Dom's reaction. He ought to have prepared better. But in fairness, she hadn't seen it coming herself.

Rafe stood, walking across to his father and sitting beside him, placing his hand on his arm. 'It's about the dream, but it's not good news. Giorgi isn't pregnant.'

'You say she never get the *bambino*?' Tears now glistened in faded eyes.

Giorgi looked away. If she cried too . . .

Rafe shook his head. 'Pa, we're desperately sorry. We waited to tell you until you were stronger, and you are now.' He gripped Dom's shoulders. 'You are an old man. You're in good shape. You have so much to look forward to. We've secured the first half of the dream against the odds. Can you settle for that?'

'No *bambinos*. Never? Who run Salerno after we gone?'

'I meant no *bambinos* for Giorgi and me, Pa. Giorgi's going back to live in Melbourne.'

His misty eyes turned upon her. She needed that cup of coffee if only as a distraction from his questioning eyes.

'But, Bruno, he be sick with you going. It not right you leave, Giorgina.'

'Please, Pa. Giorgi's been wonderful. She wanted the merger as much as anyone. It's not her fault things didn't work out for us. To be honest, we haven't been happy together. She only agreed to stay this long for your sake.'

'You take the church vows, you cannot break them,' he said weakly.

'If you have to blame someone, blame me. But at the time we wanted to give you something to hang on to after your heart attack. Now it's time for you and me to let her go. You can do that, can't you, Pa? You're big enough, love her enough to let her go without resentment?'

Tears streamed down his cheeks. 'The church not forgive you, but I try for Bruno.'

Giorgi knelt beside him. 'Pa, we still love each other like brother and sister, and you'll always be my Papa Dom. One day Rafe will find someone he loves as a woman. You will have your *bambinos*. Please be strong, as strong as my Pa was when my Ma left. I know you can do it. Forgive us. We didn't want to hurt you.'

The old man nodded, thumping his chest with a fist. 'It always here in my heart that things not right, but I not want to think . . . I want you be my daughter, like Anna.'

'And you can see how unfair that is, can't you?' Rafe chipped in. 'She's her lovely self, and we should be grateful that she's put her life on hold for us.'

'But she your wife.'

Rafe decided against telling him the marriage had not been consummated and could one day be annulled. He really didn't want to think about that himself. For now he settled for what they'd achieved. Though obviously distressed, Pa seemed to be holding up well.

As Giorgi continued to say crooning words to Dom, Rafe called Rosa in. His tact well beyond testing, bluntly he told her Giorgi was leaving for good, and he wanted her to look after Dom while he drove his wife to the airport.

Rosa threw her hands in the air, let out a wail, 'Holy Mother,' and then suggested, 'I make the coffee, Mr. Rafe.'

Rafe was grateful for the sounds of Dom sniffing away the dampness of tears, and Rosa crashing utensils about as she filled the coffee percolator. It masked the uncomfortable silence between him and Giorgi. It was over, and it had gone better than he had hoped, so why didn't he feel relieved?

Rosa handed the cups of hot, syrupy liquid around. Giorgi moved across to the window. The sunshine danced across her glossy dark hair; hair he'd often yearned to run his hand through. His mind journeyed back to the days, to the years when she would no longer be here. Of the flights of fancy he had had about her which would no longer rank as even possibilities. And he realized that telling Dom about their separation wouldn't be the most gut-wrenching experience for him. That was yet to happen as he came to terms with not having Giorgi around.

Emptiness settled in the pit of his stomach. The coffee burned down his throat.

13

Giorgi stood at the reception desk of her restaurant, glancing down at the bookings for the evening. The business was doing well. But she hadn't been able to recapture the magic she once felt about it. It had a lot to do with Nathan.

After returning to the city, she immediately immersed herself back into running the restaurant to keep her mind occupied and her thoughts in long-term storage.

'I'm back,' she'd announced. 'Thanks, Nat, for taking over while I was away.'

'You're here permanently? Are you alone?' Her stark declaration had shaken him, his jaw had jutted.

'Fancy free and ready to go.'

'Do you plan to sack Kylie? She's our hostess.'

'Let me think about it.'

Slowly she realized, in her eagerness to satisfy her own needs, she'd forgotten everyone else's. She hadn't thought her reappearance through. The once harmonious working relationship with the staff became strained, tense-filled, particularly with Nathan. Though later she apologized for her boots-and-all approach, and he accepted it, she sensed that beneath his calm exterior resentment bubbled away.

He'd enjoyed being not only head chef, but also the boss. Why wouldn't he? She also suspected he enjoyed having Kylie around. That they may have been seeing one another outside working hours. It didn't squeeze even a modicum of envy from her. Nat deserved to find a woman, and if Kylie were that person . . . She decided to keep the new hostess on as her assistant.

But the buzz she once felt from being in charge didn't return. The goal posts had shifted in her absence, and she noticed that the very competent Nathan without even trying, made her feel like an appendage.

You're allowing your imagination too much freedom, she assured herself. You're still getting over the last few months.

Tonight, she looked up as Nat surged through the door, as if he'd been prompted by the stage manager to enter left when she raised her eyes.

'Hi, Giorgi. You're here early again. Can't stay away from the place, eh?' He wasn't as tall or as strong as Rafe, his brown hair flopping across his forehead, he had a rather forced cheerfulness and optimism. Funny, but she'd never noticed the color of his eyes, except they couldn't be described as enigmatic, fiery or gentle, always beautifully dark. And he couldn't be described any more as obliging or anxious to please her.

'Of course, the restaurant is my life,' she said quietly, as he kissed her cheek, and then perused the booking list over her shoulder.

'You should get out more. Enjoy yourself. The place can run without you, you know.'

She turned to meet his teasing eyes. His reminder hurt, ate into her confidence. Every muscle in her body seemed to tighten up. She controlled an urge to shout, *You don't have to spell it out. I know you don't need me around.*

Instead she said in a husky voice, 'I've been through the menu. It sounds delicious. Would you like me to check out the table allocations?'

Nat raised his brows. 'You might have a union walkout on your hands if you do. That's Kylie's job. Have you thought any more about buying the new restaurant you mentioned?'

Giorgi raised her hands airily. 'It's still on the drawing board of my mind.' She'd made the mistake of discussing the idea of opening a second restaurant in the Nicholson Street cafe culture strip, and he'd embraced it with tear-away enthusiasm. He wanted to be a partner.

Originally it seemed like a good plan, but his managerial attitude, though he obviously tried to curb it, irritated her and she'd felt compelled to do a rethink. Clearly they couldn't both run things and work effectively alongside one another.

Her last partnership had taken her on an emotional ferris wheel ride — over and over, stomach-churning, adrenaline running. Not that her feelings for Nathan were remotely like those she had for Rafe. Until her return she'd always enjoyed his company, and they had the restaurant in common, but now she didn't quite trust him. He'd asked her again if she'd marry him once her divorce came through.

It wasn't a romantic proposal, just a simple statement. It occurred to her he may have asked hoping it was his ticket to a share in the restaurant rather than in her life. But, heaven help her, she'd started forming conspiracy theories for so many things, perhaps because she'd had experience. She and Rafe had conspired over their marriage, she thought, with an empty feeling inside.

Nat didn't know, of course, that her marriage was to be annulled, or that, for some reason, Rafe had made no attempt yet to set this in train. So much for her hopes that he and Serena were in a hurry to get together.

Don't let your mind wander off, she told herself as she closed the book, strolling across to one of the freshly laid tables.

'So when are you going to make up your mind?'

Her eyes narrowed. Being pushed on the issue wasn't helping his cause.

'I'm not ready to get married again,' she snapped.

'I'll take that as a no then. But I happen to be talking about the Nicholson Street place.'

She clipped a strand of hair over one ear, felt a rush of heat up her neck. How could she have been so confused?

'Don't pressure me, Nathan. You'll be the first to hear when I've decided. And yes, you can take the other matter as closed.' Pretending a cool she didn't have, idly she picked up a serviette and replaced it at a slightly different angle on the table.

'If you keep me waiting too long, I might decide to go it alone.' She looked up to find mocking eyes glinting in her direction.

'Fair enough.' She couldn't afford to lose him, but she hated being fenced in. That was one reason why she'd loved this restaurant, given her career its head and gone for it. It was why she'd come back with such purpose and energy. It was supposed to fill her life, her mind with challenges, help her get her head together again. Submerge her thoughts of Rafe, of loving him.

She hadn't anticipated Nathan's discontent. It told her how out of touch her thinking was.

As she strolled off to the cloakroom she smarted at the mistake she'd made over the marriage proposal. Perhaps the way to go was a second restaurant, with

Nathan managing it. But where would she get a chef for Giorgina's? People came to indulge themselves on his delicious foods, the tempting menus he presented. She, as hostess, wearing boutique dresses, offering a welcoming smile and a guarantee of good food and good service, wasn't the major player in the success of the place.

Taking a deep breath, she changed into her hostess gear for the evening, brushed up her hair, and applied light make-up. The decision would have to wait for tomorrow, maybe next week, maybe never. Damn it, since coming back from the Bend, nothing seemed straightforward, simple. Her mind fogged up with uncertainty every time she tried to be assertive. Somebody or something always got in her way. She'd lost the ability to be decisive.

Somehow she got through the night, and the next one, without snapping at Nathan for his unsubtle hints that she interfered in running the restaurant. But by Sunday lunch, her patience was all used up. When he chipped at her for coming into his kitchen too often, she retorted harshly, 'Whose kitchen did you say it was?'

The staff looked up, then hastily returned to their jobs. She colored and hurried out. The kitchen door flapped behind her, its sound blanking out his reply. She stood at the reception desk, her knuckles white as they gripped its edge. *Get yourself together Giorgi. You're on a collision course with Nathan. If you're not careful you'll lose him and your business. Buy the new restaurant, take it over and leave this one to him. These days it feels more like his anyway.*

A waiter placed a small silver saucer bearing a credit card and an account on the desk. Giorgi attended to it with an automatic smile. As each client left, her smile returned, followed by, 'Come again soon.' But she was operating like a robot when once even actions as small as these induced a flow of adrenaline, a desire to impress and encourage diners back.

Tomorrow she'd call the estate agent back. Ask if he could show her any coffee houses for sale along the trendy Fitzroy or St. Kilda strips. She took a deep breath. Hopefully a new restaurant, one she'd refurbish, stamp with her own particular style, would encourage her to set goals again, give some impetus to her life.

She forced herself to do one more thing before the restaurant closed that night. Entering the kitchen, she called so that the staff would hear, 'Nat, I apologize for getting in your way earlier and sounding bitchy. From now on the kitchen is out of limits to me while the place is open, and if I barge in, or start pushing my weight around, I'm giving you permission to turn me around and push me out.' She gestured towards the staff with her arms, smiling. 'And you have witnesses.'

They laughed uneasily. Tears stung the backs of her eyes. It cost her, but she and Nathan couldn't go on sniping at one another. It was bad for morale.

Everyone probably sensed the tense atmosphere between them — the staff certainly, possibly the clients.

Nathan came to her side, lowering his voice. 'We have to talk.'

'Whenever.' Weary, she felt like sighing, asking if it couldn't wait until later, but putting off problems didn't solve anything. In her business life, she tried to adhere to the old maxim, 'Do it once and do it right.'

'Now.' He led her back into the empty restaurant, indicating a table. As they sat down, he said, 'Giorgi, it's your kitchen. I'm glad you reminded me of that earlier. After managing Giorgina's all those months, I guess I find it hard to forget the boss is back.'

Giorgi couldn't help noticing, when he smiled, that his eyes didn't hold their usual teasing luminescence. She placed her hand over his, intending to apologize again for the clumsy way she'd handled her return, but her senses alerted to his soft, spongy hands. She began to compare them with

Rafe's. Long, lean, tanned, work-hardened hands. Beautiful to the touch.

She forced her attention back to Nathan. He was staring at her. 'You're not with me, Giorgi. What's troubling you? I can tell you've got something on your mind.'

She withdrew her hand. 'I'm unsettled. This has been the year from hell for me, one I'm trying to forget. First I lost my family, then my marriage failed. It's been a rough ride. But what I said back there in the kitchen, I meant. I'm not excusing myself for the cavalier way I swept back here and took over again. I've treated you shabbily. Are we okay now?'

'Want Uncle Nat's advice?' The teasing light flashed back into his eyes.

'I'm not sure that I do. I can't guarantee to act on it.'

'The sooner you get your divorce the better you'll feel. Don't let it hang over your head forever. Get it out of the way. And for my encore, why not buy another restaurant, one that's a bit run down? You can build it up. Redecorate, refurnish. You're good at that kind of thing, and it'll give you a whole new and exciting project to focus on. At the moment that's missing from your life.'

'My, Nat, you're in the wrong business. You should be a mind reader. Not ten minutes ago I was thinking identical thoughts.'

'Don't leave them dangling as thoughts. Take some action.'

'I've already decided on a new place. Would you be awfully disappointed if we didn't go into partnership? You'd have free rein here. Just as you did while I was living at River Bend.' Did she detect a cloud shadow his eyes?

'I was hoping for a double partnership, but I guess that's a pipe dream?'

'Afraid so. I've overdosed on marriage, Nat. I'm still recovering. I think it's only fair to tell you that it's off the agenda.'

'What happened, Giorgi? I hope the swine didn't . . . '

'He's my best friend,' she cut in,

unwilling for him to think ill of Rafe. 'What about you? I had an idea you and Kylie might have been an item during my absence.'

He laughed. 'She's a nice kid, but there's no chemistry. Like you and that husband of yours, eh? No chemistry.'

What a damned awful joke!

★   ★   ★

A brisk autumn wind agitated the fallen leaves from the giant elm trees lining the path's verge. An abandoned empty drink can rattled along the street as Giorgi walked to her home from the tram stop.

As she planned her evening, for the first time in ages, pleasure rippled through her. She'd kept the property sections of the two major newspapers, and would search through them tonight for a new business opportunity. But first she'd turn on the CD, light the fire — she hadn't done that since her return — and toast crumpets. She patted her hair back into place as she reached her gate, a spring in her step.

The minute she opened the door of the house, the aroma of wood smoke met her. She paused, alarmed, puzzled. Somebody was here. Somebody . . . dare she hope? Taking a deep breath, silently she unloaded her shopping bag in the hall, slipped off her shoes and in bare feet tip-toed into the living room. A fire burned in the grate. From behind her, hands clapped about her eyes.

'Guess who?'

She stood very still, fighting with herself, with a traitorous heart which wanted to cry out for joy when she should have felt only anger. He'd let himself into her home, made himself at home, lit her fire, as if he still had a claim over her. And just when she'd made a positive move to reshape her life.

But her heart had its way. How could it be otherwise?

'Rafe,' she cried as his hands fell away. She turned back to him, wrapping her arms about his neck, briefly placing her lips to his cheek. 'It's so good to see you. How long has it been?'

'Too long.' His dark eyes gleamed. 'It's better than good to see you. It's fantastic. I hope you don't mind. I still had the key you gave me. I wanted to get the house warm for you.'

She tugged off her coat, flinging it across a chair, moving, doing, trying to get herself together. He'd come, of course, to ask about the divorce. He'd finally decided to marry Serena. Emptiness replaced the joy she at first felt.

'Why didn't you use the electric heaters?' she snapped, unable to overcome her irrational disappointment.

He raised dark brows. 'I know how you like your romantic little fire.'

Odd that she'd planned a fire herself, she thought vaguely, avoiding his eyes by staring into the flames, refusing the surge of desire she knew his smile would bring. It almost overwhelmed her that their separation had done nothing, absolutely nothing to change her feelings for him.

How often had she tried to bury her love for him beneath layers of common-sense, and how often had she failed? Now it resurfaced with all its beauty and all its risks.

'Is Pa Dom okay?' she managed.

'He's doing surprisingly well. He sends his love. Rosa, too.'

She tried to close out the memories of River Bend, 'I'm hungry. Can I get something for you?'

'You're shivering. Sit down and warm yourself. I can rustle up a snack.'

Giorgi flopped onto the sofa without any urging to take the strain from her wobbly legs. 'Thanks. There are some crumpets in my shopping bag. I dropped it in the hall. I was going to . . .'

'Toast them by the fire? Remember the last time we did that?' Without waiting for a response, he turned towards the hall, adding. 'I'll bring in the toasting forks. You can make a start while I put on the kettle.'

Giorgi leaned towards the fire. The

flames licked along the split logs, dancing a flamenco as they reached the ends. Like her feelings.

Soon he returned to the sitting room with the crumpets and forks. Her eyes feasted on him. It was so damned good to have him here, and yet so wrong.

Rafe made his way back to the kitchen. Her reaction to his arrival had given him a spark of hope. As he reached down the mugs and warmed the teapot, he searched his mind for the right words to say. God, he'd missed her. Just now when she threw her arms about him, it was all he could manage not to crush her to him, to cover her with kisses. Tell her he loved her deeply. Beyond his understanding. So much so, that he had been fooled by the old men's dream that had directed him onto a detour down the wrong road.

Once, he had let her go and thought with arrogance that the property could fill the gap. But he'd been God-awful wrong. And now he was back to fight for her. Bugger the dream.

She would call the shots, set the agenda. He'd even give up the warmth and open spaces of the Sunset Country to live in the city, in this dark little house, if that's what it took. His life was incomplete, an empty shell, without her beside him.

He carried the tea tray into the sitting room and set it on the low coffee table. For perhaps half an hour they toasted crumpets, buttered and honeyed them, poured tea, chatted. Easy going on the outside. But by the minute he grew anxious, impatient. Soon she'd ask questions. He had to find the right words.

'You didn't say why you're in Melbourne, Rafe. If it's got something to do with the annulment . . . ' She ran the tip of her tongue over full, sensual lips, before patting her mouth with a tissue. He remembered that once, long ago, when those lovely lips had surrendered to him. They had been dancing in her restaurant. At the time he wondered if the kiss had meant something to her, but had failed to come up with an answer. There were times when he'd fantasized about that kiss.

How had he managed such self-control all those months, when she slept so close and the heat in his body cried out for her? By blanking her out, calling on memories of Anna. But nothing really worked. Always Giorgi's, not Anna's, image came up when he tapped the keys of his memory. His lovely little dude.

She filled the silence. 'If you're planning to marry Serena . . . '

He laughed tauntingly. 'You didn't fool me. I knew what you were up to there.'

'She's in love with you, Rafe. Anyone could read it in her eyes.' Giorgi brushed crumbs from her trousers, pushing back against the sofa. 'She'd make a splendid wife. She'd give you and Pa Guardiani *bambinos*.'

'I've already got a wife and Serena is going steady with a guy now, thank goodness. The old hero-worship was a bit of a drag for a while.'

'I know how it feels to hero worship. It can be very painful.'

He nodded. 'But you grew up and found out what an ordinary bloke I am.'

'I've never thought of you as ordinary.'

'How *have* you thought of me, Giorgi?'

As he lifted himself from the floor rug onto the sofa he saw color sweep across her cheeks. She brushed hair back from her face and moved uneasily to her side of the sofa.

'Oh, a touch hot tempered, arrogant sometimes, obstinate when you choose, generous on occasions — the ideal brother-in-law.' Her lips arced into a gentle smile.

'Not the ideal husband?'

'Definitely not. You scored a big fat zero there.' She'd tried to joke, but her voice didn't hold up.

Get on with it, he told himself. Stop procrastinating. He closed the space between them with one deft movement, put his arm about her shoulders, tilted her face to his by cupping her chin in his hand. 'Is there any chance for us, Giorgi? Could we try again? This time as husband and wife.'

Her eyes shadowed. 'As husband and wife? You mean sleep together?'

'Yes.'

Giorgi brushed aside his hand. 'How would that change anything, except satisfy your sexual needs?' Her voice took on a hard edge.

'And yours? You have them, too. Don't you? It's there, drawing us together and we're denying it.' *Damn it, that wasn't what he meant to say.*

'Only for one man, and he's always been in love with someone else.'

A spark flew from the fire, settling on the rug. He released Giorgi's shoulder and trod it out, then faced her, narrowing his eyes. 'You've been in love all this time and not told me? Who's the man? He must be crazy not to want you.'

Her laugh had a cynical ring to it. 'He doesn't know.'

The disappointment almost robbed him of words. She loved someone. Probably that chef guy who worked for her. He was too late.

'Aren't we a couple of fools,' he managed to say.

'I thought you'd press me to find out about the man.'

'When are you planning to tell him?'

'Probably never.'

He didn't care that she didn't love him. He wanted her to be his wife. 'So there's a chance for us?'

'I thought we'd already made that decision. I don't understand why you're going on about it?'

'Things are different now. Once you questioned whether a marriage between Anna and me would have worked. The cold, hard facts are, it didn't have a hope in Hades. We'd have been miserable. We were chalk and cheese. I'm surprised I only started thinking seriously about it a year or so ago.'

Giorgi's eyes grew wide. 'But you were wildly in love with her. You can't deny it.'

He shook his head slowly. 'I was conditioned by the family. Infatuated. My manhood flattered by the knowledge that a sexy woman the men flocked around was promised to me. Besides, the wedding wouldn't have taken place.'

'Well no, because of the accident.'

'Not exactly. Giorgi. I haven't told you this before for the best reasons, but I should have.

She slipped back into the sofa, her fingers laced tightly across her flat stomach.

'The night Anna died I went looking for her towards the end of the party and found her waiting on your back verandah with two packed suitcases. She laughed in my face, told me she was leaving with Greg Salter, the owner of a chain of hotels, one of them at the Bend. I shouldn't be telling you this . . . '

She dragged in a breath. 'Go on. I want to know the truth.'

'She was your sister. I don't want to spoil your memories of her.'

'What happened that night?' she prompted gently. 'Did my Pa know?'

'I knew *I* couldn't talk her out of it. I don't think I even wanted to. I'd lost all respect for her by then, but I couldn't let her sneak away under cover of darkness the way your Ma did, without saying goodbye. I insisted she tell her father. We went to Bruno together because I didn't trust her to go alone. Your Pa suggested they take a drive together, talk about it. I think he hoped to get her to change her mind, but fate had other plans. They didn't come home alive, and Greg Salter went back to his wife.'

'It's so . . . oh, Rafe, it's awful. My poor Pa, poor misguided Anna. I wonder what happened in that car?' she murmured, dabbing at her eyes.

'Does it matter now?'

'And you've lived with the knowledge

all this time. Why didn't you feel you could share it with me?'

'She was your sister. You loved her. How could I destroy the illusion once she had gone?'

'You loved her, too.'

He shook his head. 'Not for a long time, probably not ever. She only knew one way to live and that was to take.'

'And yet you were prepared to marry her.'

'Yes. I wasn't about to let her take the dream away from Dom and Bruno. I hoped she'd settle down.' He laughed harshly. 'Super optimist, eh?'

'And now . . . did you say you've really fallen in love?' she whispered. 'I'm pleased for you. If it's not Serena, who's the . . . ' Her voice faltered. 'Who's the woman?'

He smiled down at her, indulging himself. 'It happened a long while ago but I refused to acknowledge it. That damned dream kept getting in the way, steering me off in the wrong direction.'

He felt her start. She turned her eyes

355

up to him. They were wide, puzzled. She dug him in the ribs.

'Well . . . '

'She loved the vineyards, used to come out to watch me work. She loved the Bend, only she hasn't actually admitted it to herself.' He tilted her chin with his index finger. 'I was never truly in love with Anna. Not the way I love you to the very depth of my soul. Can you find it in your heart to love me, just a little?'

Giorgi met his smoldering dark eyes, her heart on hold. 'You're in love . . . with me? How can I be so . . . so lucky. You love me?' she stammered.

'Deeply, everlastingly, with all my being. You're my lifeline, my reason for living.' His lips brushed her cheeks. 'My sweet wife.'

Her eyes were misty as she looked up at him. 'Sometimes I thought you'd guess how I felt about you.' She brushed her soft hand down his cheek, over his eyes. 'Such beautiful eyes, such a beloved face. I've always loved you.'

'Why didn't you tell me?'

'You were Anna's man, and my big brother.'

'We should have stopped pretending years ago and given in to our true feelings. Don't you see, sweetheart, we were meant to be together. At home, after you left, I'd sit outside for hours thinking it all through. I could feel you beside me on those still nights, the quiet, open companionship we shared, and the brightest stars, as I looked up at them, were your magical eyes watching over me, telling me everything would come right in the end.' He leaned forward, placing his lips gently to her mouth. 'I missed you, Giorgi.'

She sat very still, her emotions scrunched up like a worry ball between strong fingers. Did she dare to believe that he had fallen in love with her? Is that what he was saying? Or was it only that he missed her?

'Your lips taste of honey,' she said tightly.

'Your lips taste of sweetness. Have you missed me?'

She nodded. 'Like crazy.'

'Giorgi, my beautiful wife. Can we give the marriage another try?' he whispered, taking her into his arms, kissing her throat, nibbling at her ear. 'I love you.'

At last she gave way, breathed in the scent of him, and released her heart to love him freely. As she twined her arms about his neck, he claimed her mouth, this time with an intensity that sent desire torching into every fiber of her body.

Such tenderness, such exquisite tension, such joy.

They eased to the floor. 'I've loved you all my life,' she whispered, 'and I never dreamed this moment would come.'

The fire spat and crackled as they discovered one another for the first time and made love.

★   ★   ★

Giorgi woke suddenly. And as suddenly realized her husband lay beside her, a strong, bare arm thrown across the duvet cover, his black hair disordered across the pink pillow case. If she gently eased back the covers, she would see him once again, beautiful in his nakedness. For the last time?

Where did she go from here? Back to River Bend? Back to being his wife? His real wife. As she slipped quietly out of bed, a shiver of excitement scudded through her. To indulge herself, get her fix every day by making love with him? He said he loved her. He sounded as if he loved her. She believed he loved her. So did anything stand in their way?

Not Anna. Of that she now felt certain. Once she had judged him obsessed with her sister. Now, she realized her own feelings were akin to an obsession. If they hadn't been, she'd have picked up the vibes, interpreted his moods differently, whenever Anna entered their conversations. She'd have sensed his growing disaffection with her sister.

Yet still she felt plagued by uncertainties.

The phone shrilled into the silence. She glanced at her watch, blinked. Ten o'clock. To avoid waking Rafe, she threw on a robe, hurried to stem the demanding ring, speaking quietly into the receiver.

'It's Nathan. I've been thinking about your plan to buy another place. Did you go through the property pages of the papers?'

'Not yet. I gave myself the night off and slept in.'

'Last night at the pub I met an old mate. He's just come back from England. He's an excellent chef, and he'll be job hunting in the next week or two. I mentioned you. You should talk to him straight away, Giorgi, if you're interested.'

She jotted down the name and contact number. 'Got it. Thanks,' she mumbled.

'You don't sound keen. Have you changed your mind again?'

Giorgi didn't like the way he said 'again', but that was unfair. He wasn't to know of the life-changing happenings of last night, or that her business plans for the future were on hold for the time being.

'I'll talk to him, but not today. I'm still ambivalent about buying another restaurant.'

She swallowed as she saw Rafe lounging against the entrance, his lean, fit body naked, except for a pair of jocks.

'Good morning, wife.' He said softly, sensually.

Giorgi held her breath as he came closer, longing to feel his arms about her.

'If you're thinking of buying another business, forget it.' He grinned. Then he folded her to his broad, muscled chest, looking down at her with gleaming dark eyes, nibbling at her ear. She burned with desire to respond, to draw him closer into her, but a small voice in her head cautioned her. He'd reminded her just now that if she returned to Salerno she'd lose her identity again. The idea swamped her with uncertainty.

'You look hot stuff in your jocks,' she said brightly, 'but it's freezing in here. You'll catch cold. Go get some clothes on while I turn on the heaters.' Gently she pushed him away.

He reached for her again. 'I was hoping you'd warm me. Come back to bed. You know what exercise does for you.' As his lips fell to her bare throat, his hand slipped beneath her robe, cupping her breast. And alive with passion, her body cried out to capitulate. But his demand for her to forget buying another restaurant echoed over and over in her mind. No consultation, no discussion.

With a groan she twisted from his grasp.

'God, Giorgi, you can't get me worked up like this and push me aside. That was a game your sister liked to play. What the hell's the matter with you?' Impatience glinted in his dark eyes.

'Every time you touch me, I want you. But I'm not fool enough to sign myself over to you body and soul to be ordered about and controlled. If I want to buy another restaurant, I'll buy one.'

He threw his arms into the air, his eyes lit with fire. 'Buy another bloody restaurant if that's what it takes to make you happy. Make it more complicated for us to be together, by all means. It's one thing to be independent, another to be willful. A marriage is supposed to be a partnership.' And he swung around, storming from the room.

14

Giorgi shivered, switched on the heater and stood toasting herself. But the warmth failed to reach into her heart. She stopped thinking altogether, staring blankly at the door.

Minutes later, Rafe reappeared, a towel flung over one shoulder, the fire of anger in his eyes burnt out. 'I'm taking a cold shower. Care to join me?'

'Ask me later. I'm not that hot any more.'

He moved into the room. 'I can soon fix that.'

She put up her arm. 'Keep your distance, Rafe. This is serious stuff we're dealing with, and I won't let you hijack my emotions. Being Italian doesn't give you the right to take over my life. I have my own goals, and I intend to achieve them.'

'Giorgi, Giorgi, Giorgi,' he stretched

his open palms towards her. 'Why do you always have to fight me? You know I don't mean it. I speak first and think second. It's my way. I thought you understood.'

When he grinned, she always found it hard not to join him and put aside the issue between them. Today there was far too much at stake. 'But sometimes you do mean it and I'm not a mind-reader. Have your shower and don't come in here again until you're wearing clothes. Then we talk. In the altogether, you're a dangerous man to be around, Rafe Guardiani.'

He straightened his back, clicked his heels together and saluted. 'Gotcha, Mrs. Guardiani.' His bare feet padded over the carpet to the sound of her laughter.

As she watched him disappear, she wrestled with an urge to call him back, fling her arms around him and tell him she didn't give a damn about a second restaurant. Without him, even one restaurant was too many. But it wouldn't have solved anything. The doubts and the problems would inevitably resurface.

Giorgi listened for the sound of the shower before she returned to the bedroom where she dressed, tidied up, and then made her way into the kitchen. She had coffee brewing, bread in the toaster, and the radio on for the news when he put his head around the door.

'Can anyone come in?'

She smiled. 'No. But you're not anyone.'

Listening to the news helped her get through the next fifteen minutes, and gave them a safe source of conversation. They'd had some much needed rain in the Sunset Country, the Independent politician for their area would vote in Parliament for further subsidized electronic services, the state gallery had managed a coup — an exhibition of classical European paintings.

But when he stood and walked across to the bench, asking, 'More coffee?' she knew the time had come to make her last decision about life with Rafe.

'Thanks.' She was about to offer to make it when he said, 'You go inside I've lit your romantic little fire. I'll bring in the drinks.'

She sat at the table, stiff, tense, her mind alert. 'It's not safe in there. I'm not safe from you. We talk out here.'

'Giorgi,' he began, 'I'm in love with you. Have been for most of my life. But we were all sun-struck by the bloody dream. Anyone with any eyes could see how drawn I was to you, how compatible we were, how comfortable together. Anyone but the Rintoli's and the Guardiani's. You do love me?'

'Yes,' she whispered. 'Everyone but me suffered sunstroke from the dream. I knew I loved you from the day I started growing breasts. But that doesn't mean I'm willing to drop everything and come back to the Bend. That's what my first stint as your wife showed me. I suppose I take after my mother. I can't idle the days away. I can't waste my education or suppress my urge to do challenging things.'

'Wouldn't babies keep you busy?'

The word babies tugged at her heart. Rafe's babies. She dropped her eyelids for a second, an image flashing into her head, and she almost answered yes, it would be enough. But she paused long enough to take a deep breath and found the strength to say, 'I'd want our children, two, maybe three, but motherhood as a career wouldn't work for me. I'd be moody, bad tempered. That's how I am. And if you can't go along with that it won't work for either of us.'

Her fingers entwined, her hands resting on the table. He covered them. 'I've thought about it a lot and I have an answer. I'm ready to give up Salerno and come live with you here if that's what it takes.'

Giorgi gasped. 'You'd do that for me?' Her fingers sweated beneath his touch.

'I can't live without you. I tried and it didn't work. You were always on my mind. I'm willing to give city life a go. We could go to the football, the theater. Who knows, I might like it.'

She tried to laugh off his magnificent gesture. 'You'd hate it,' she said, tears blurring her vision. 'You make me feel incredibly humble, and a cold, selfish bitch.'

'Don't cry, sweet wife.' His fingers reached to catch the tears as they began to flow down her cheeks. 'You gave up everything at our first attempt at marriage. Now it's my turn. I don't want you to feel guilty or selfish. This is my idea.'

His understanding, his generosity of heart made it harder to control her weeping. Through her tears, she stammered. 'I love you . . . I love you, Rafe. That's why I'd never ask or expect you to give up your heritage. You'd languish in this environment. You'd change. I love you as you are. I wouldn't want to change you in the smallest way.' She shook her head. 'I can't accept your offer.'

'Think about it. Don't decide now. Give yourself time. I'll go home, make my arrangements for Mario to take over the place, bring back a few clothes. Why don't we try for six months? If it doesn't work, then we'll call it quits. Don't slam the door on me before you've given it a chance.'

Wiping away the remnants of tears with a tissue, she put the coffee cup to her mouth, tasting the strong, bitter liquid. 'This is your best friend talking now. Within days you'll be pacing the floor, within a week stir-crazy. The Sunset Country's in your blood.'

'Are you forgetting it's in yours, too, and you managed to move on successfully. If you're suggesting I don't have that kind of grit . . . ?'

Giorgi looked down at her hands. He was getting to her. Slowly eroding her determination to do what was clearly going to be right for both of them in the end.

'You're forgetting that I moved on years ago. Besides, I always planned to leave the Bend. You always planned to reach your old age up there.'

He rose, stood with his back to the heater, appraising her with gentle dark eyes, eyes that were irresistible. 'Think of it, Giorgi. You and me together. We can do anything together. You've taken risks before. Go for it now.'

'This would be the greatest risk of all.' She sighed, standing up and gripping the back of the chair, wrestling still with the urge to chance it and fall into his arms. She had no idea where the strength came from, but she heard herself say. 'We both know living down here would crush your spirit. I can't stand around and watch that happen. You mean everything to me.'

'You're telling me it's over before it's hardly begun.' He narrowed his eyes, pacing the floor, his hands deep into his pockets.

'We still have today.'

He came to her in one stride. 'Oh my God, Giorgi,' he moaned. And clasping her to him, he kissed her, his lips caressing her body, his hands running through her hair and stroking her thighs. They sank onto the sofa and made love as if there were no tomorrow.

15

Giorgi felt listless, off color. For days she'd wandered about lightheaded, machine-like, discharging her duties at the restaurant, smiling at the clients, balancing the books, keeping Nathan onside.

She'd consulted a real estate agent, but didn't follow up on his property recommendations. Outside the cold easterlies of mid-winter tugged at her coat and hair. Inside her little house, the only sunshine in her day came when Rafe rang.

At every call he promised it would be his last at her insistence, yet when the phone rang she sprang to answer it with an energy which eluded her at all other times. And when he hung up, the hole in her life seemed to grow bigger and blacker. She felt sure he knew his advantage, and he worked on it. And she lacked the toughness to change her address or her phone number to close him out of her life altogether.

'I'm coming down for a conference at the school of agriculture next week. Can I stay with you?' he said when she answered the phone. 'Promise. I won't get in your way.'

He couldn't hear her heart quicken or see the joy lighting her eyes.

'Are you still on the line?' he asked.

'Yes. Of course you're welcome to stay.' Her voice quivered. She came close to adding, *I want you to get in my way. I want to get in yours. I want you, full stop. I'm an empty shell of a person without you.*

The week crept by, each minute measuring an hour. Giorgi busied herself doing a winter spring clean. She employed a cheerful tradesman to paint her little kitchen in off-white, picking out the woodwork in sunshine yellow, to give it a light, airy feel. She hung new curtains, had a ton of chopped firewood delivered, as if she were preparing for his homecoming.

And all the while thoughts of last winter spun in her mind. That's where it had all started. When Rafe had arrived on her doorstep to ask her to marry him. It was a night forever imprinted on her mind. It had brought uncertainty, ambivalence, separation, love. Until then, she'd had everything under control.

But you couldn't flick a year out of your life with an electrostatic duster, as if it were a buildup of ash from the winter fires. She knew the truth. She just had to come to terms with it. Functioning without Rafe had become well-nigh impossible. An answer might be to spend alternative weeks in Melbourne and River Bend so they could be together. Her thoughts stalled there. It was ludicrous to think she could go back to River Bend occasionally to be a part-time wife to Rafe. It would practically be a stoning offense in the Italian community, she mused, smiling briefly. Maybe a compromise.

They could meet half way. Bendigo?

She was stretching for the stars, but reaching nothing tangible to ease her mind and solve their dilemma. Her mental meanderings through the possibilities always ended at a no-through road sign. *Bottom line? You have to go back to the Bend. Have to give up your career. Life without your husband is no life at all.*

On the morning Rafe was due, she went shopping — the pharmacy, the supermarket — and hurried home, excitement stirring her step.

★　★　★

Rafe dropped his bag from his shoulder and was about to put his key in the lock when the door flew open. He folded Giorgi to him, kissing her, murmuring into her hair, 'How is my sweet wife?'

Next he held her at arm's length, gazing at her lovely face. Her cheeks glowed, her blue eyes shone. But she looked thinner. 'You haven't been eating enough pasta,' he said, retrieving his bag, slipping his arm around her waist as they entered the house. 'Is that wood smoke I can smell? You've lit the fire?'

'For our reunion. The coffee's on and the crumpets at the ready. Put your bag in the bedroom, then go warm yourself in the sitting room. I'll bring in a tray.'

'The bedroom? Does that mean what I think it does?' His glance caught the mischievous spark in her eyes, the curve of full lips.

'We're married aren't we?' She turned away then.

His first heated urge was to go after her, carry her to the bedroom, peel off her clothes, feel again the texture of her skin, smell the fragrance of her body . . . He cautioned himself. Keep it cool. No need to rush. Get it right. He had a surprise for her, but he had to do it right.

He dropped his bag in the bedroom and returned to the kitchen. 'Nice,' he said, glancing around the freshly painted walls. 'Are you planning to have the rest of the place painted?' If she were, did it mean she had long-term plans to stay put? It slightly dented his hopes.

'No. This was a spur-of-the-moment thing. When I knew you were coming, I kind of felt excited, and got stuck into a few things. I've been pretty listless since you left.'

He crossed to stand at her back, placing his arms around her waist, his cheek to hers. 'You still love me?'

She raised her hand, brushing it down his other cheek. 'You know I'm nuts about you. I always have been.' Then she turned, looking into his eyes, and at once they both said, 'I've got something exciting to tell . . . ' before breaking into laughter.

'You first,' she said, lightly touching her lips to his.

She seemed skittish, excited, provocative. At seeing him? Something more was switching her on. Whatever, it upped the heat in his body. He didn't know how much longer he could control the surge of need rifling through him, but he managed to say, 'I think we should sit down to discuss what I have to tell you. It could knock you off your feet.'

Her brows winged, she tilted her head, 'Wow. That good? Let's talk by the fire.'

She picked up the tray and presented it to him. 'Our fire,' she said, again with a mischievous curve of her lips, blow-torch blue eyes burning.

In the sitting room, she flopped on to the mat in front of the flames, patting the space next to her.

'I'm not joining you,' he said, easing onto the sofa. 'I can't get distracted before I put my proposal to you. Otherwise it'll get tangled up with our emotional needs.'

'Oh,' she said, twisting around to face him. 'Isn't anything more important than our needs?'

'Don't look at me like that, Giorgi.'
'What?'

'You've got the hots for me.'

'Might have. But you're obviously not in any hurry to take up my invitation.'

'I can promise you'll get badly burned if you sit close to me.'

'So what's holding you up?' She rested her head against his legs. Heat scorched into his groin.

'You know Pa and I have talked about setting up a winery on the vineyard?'

She shrugged. 'Huh, you've been talking about it forever.'

'We didn't have the finances. We have now. It's to be a tourist attraction, with a tasting area and . . . ' He threw up his arms. 'And here's the best part . . . a restaurant. Your restaurant — Bruno's, or Guardiani's, or Giorgi's — whatever name you choose. You will take it over and run it, won't you?'

She took his hand, pressing him to slide down beside her. The tea tray overturned with a crash, water splashing across the floor. 'Ignore it,' she said, slipping his arms around her. 'Rafe, do you mean it?'

'I don't know why it wasn't on the drawing board years ago,' he whispered into her hair, hugging closer to her.

'I thought about it at one stage, but then I couldn't have lived in the Bend while you and Anna were lovers. Later I bought my own little place, enjoyed it, and well, it went out of my mind.'

He tucked a finger under her chin, tilting it. 'Then you like the idea?'

'Like it? It's sensational. My own restaurant at River Bend. I can already picture it overlooking the river, a wide glassed-in eating area, lawns running down to the water's edge, barbecues, tables, chairs, marquees for the bus trippers, paddle boats steaming down river bringing the more leisurely to dine.' She bubbled over with words, her eyes gleaming. 'You mean it? You'll give me my head? I design it? I engage the staff?'

'I'll give you anything you ask if you'll come home, where you belong, where I can watch over you, take care of you.'

She laughed. 'You're starting to sound like a patronizing Italian gentleman again. And you know what?

'What?'

'I don't care. I can handle it. I've had a lifetime of experience at it.'

He brushed his hand down her soft, creamy neck. 'Giorgi, I can't remember a better day.'

'It needs something more to make it perfect, and I have exactly what it needs to do that.'

'We can start making babies now.' He ran his hand inside her shift, feeling the heat, the satin smoothness of her breast. She started, moaning softly, then pushed his hand aside.

'How can I find time to plan and run my restaurant when I'm having Rintoli babies?'

He didn't understand the smirk that flashed into her eyes and drew her curved lips together.

'Babies were always part of the deal.

If they're not, *you'll* have to tell Pa there won't be any *bambinos*. I broke the last piece of bad news to him.' He laughed.

'Seriously. Are babies important to you?'

He shrugged, trying to sound nonchalant. He wanted kids, a smart little girl like Giorgi, a tough little bloke to take over Salerno one day. But if Giorgi gave the thumbs down, he could live with it. She was Mark One. Anything after that would be a bonus.

'I can't imagine life without children, but you're what I want and if you come without babies . . . ' He shrugged. 'Though I hoped with some domestic help you could plan your career around having one or two children. That's what today's women, do isn't it? But hey, if you don't think it would work . . . ' He held the palms of his hands out, 'You're calling the shots on this.'

'Then it doesn't worry you if I tell you I'm pregnant?'

Giorgi watched light leap into his

dark eyes, then fade almost as quickly, replaced by doubt.

'You're kidding me? You mean that last time we were together . . . Can it be?' He reached out to her, folded her in his arms. She heard his strong heart beat as she laid her head against his broad chest.

'Yes.' She brushed her hand along his shadowed jaw, lowering her voice. 'I'm having your baby.'

'Are you sure? How long have you known?' He kissed the palm of her hand.

'I suspected. Today I bought a test kit from the chemist.'

'Tomorrow we go see a doctor.' He placed his hand over her stomach. 'Our baby. God, Giorgi, what a bloody lovely day it's been.'

'Tomorrow you've got your conference.'

He laughed. 'There is no conference. I needed an excuse to come down.'

'You can be such a liar.'

'What a bloody perfect day it's been,'

he repeated, as if he couldn't believe it, before tilting her mouth to his and kissing her.

'One more thing,' Giorgi said between his kisses.

'Name it.' His hand stroked the shirt from her shoulder blade.

'I'd like us to renew our wedding vows. The first time we made them there was so much uncertainty. I want to say 'til death do us part' to you. I want you to know nothing can separate us now.'

'Can you make arrangements for us to do that in Melbourne?' he said as the soft pad of his thumb caressed her nipple. She cried out gently and gave herself up to him.

★   ★   ★

It took a few days for Giorgi to organize her departure from Melbourne. The doctor confirmed her pregnancy. Rafe had the look of a small boy who'd kicked the winning goal when she came out of the doctor's office with the news. They lunched in Lygon Street, but he refused her suggestion of a celebratory drink. She laughed. 'Aren't you carrying all this a bit too far?'

'You can have one glass of alcohol with your dinner at night. Not before.'

She laughed. 'You still haven't learned who's boss of this union have you?'

'Of the unimportant things, do you mean?'

★　★　★

They renewed their vows, lighting candles, holding hands, their eyes misty, as they stood before the altar in the Lady Chapel of the lovely old church in the foothills of Melbourne.

Lastly Giorgi put her house up for sale and negotiated an acceptable price for 'Giorgina's' with Nathan. This time she would leave nothing behind. Her life in the city was over.

With a heart full of joy, her baby growing inside her, her plans for her restaurant etched in her mind, she was investing her future in River Bend beside the man she had loved for a life time.

The million dollar dream had come to pass.

THE END

TO LOVE AGAIN

Catriona McCuaig

Jenny Doyle had always loved her brother in law, Jake Thomas-Harding, but when he chose to marry her sister instead, she knew it was a love that had no future. Now his wife is dead, and he asks Jenny to live under his roof to look after his little daughter. She wonders what the future holds for them all, especially when ghosts of the past arise to haunt them . . .

FINDING THE SNOWDON LILY

Heather Pardoe

Catrin Owen's father, a guide on Snowdon, shows botanists the sites of rare plants. He wants his daughter to marry Taran Davies. But then the attractive photographer Philip Meredith and his sister arrive, competing to be first to photograph the 'Snowdon Lily' in its secret location. His arrival soon has Catrin embroiled in the race, and she finds her life, as well as her heart, at stake. For the coveted prize generates treachery amongst the rivals — and Taran's jealousy . . .

KEEP SAFE THE PAST

Dorothy Taylor

Their bookshop in the old Edwardian Arcade meant everything to Jenny Wyatt and her father. But were the rumours that the arcade was to be sold to a development company true? Jenny decides to organise a protest group. Then, when darkly attractive Leo Cooper enters her life, his upbeat personality is like a breath of fresh air. But as their relationship develops, Jenny questions her judgement of him. Are her dreams of true love about to be dashed?

LEGACY OF REGRET

Jo James

When Liz Shepherd unexpectedly inherits an elderly man's considerable estate, she is persuaded it is in gratitude for her kindness to him. But doubts set in when Steve Lewis, in the guise of a reporter, challenges her good luck. Was there another reason for her legacy? And why is Steve so interested? She comes to regret her inheritance and all its uncertainties — until Steve helps her find the truth and they discover the secret of their past.